THE 6' 1" GRINCH
Tiffany White

Harlequin Books

TORONTO • NEW YORK • LONDON
AMSTERDAM • PARIS • SYDNEY • HAMBURG
STOCKHOLM • ATHENS • TOKYO • MILAN
MADRID • WARSAW • BUDAPEST • AUCKLAND

ISBN 0-373-44009-X

THE 6' 1" GRINCH

Copyright © 1996 by Anna Eberhardt

I have always adored romantic comedies because the man who can make me laugh wins my heart. And when it comes to the season of Christmas, well what's not to like about a holiday that celebrates love and involves presents! Combining the two seemed natural.

As an extroverted, impractical, extravagant Leo, I, of course, married an introverted, practical and thrifty Capricorn. Also known as a grinch. So when my editor invited me to write for the new Love & Laughter line, I was thrilled. I had plenty of personal research on the 6' 1" grinch.

On our first Christmas together my grinch gave me bake wear. I didn't say a word in front of his family, but later explained I wanted a personal gift in the future.

Our second Christmas my grinch presented me with a blender. I pitched a fit right in front of his family...only to belatedly discover the beautiful gold locket inside the blender. I'd forgotten my grinch's wry humor.

But beware of what you wish for because my reformed grinch has taken my desire for personal gifts to heart, and while I'm longing for the newest laptop computer on the market, he's happily browsing through Victoria's Secret.

—Tiffany White

To Lance and Millicent Thomure

Thanks to Nancy DuMeyer—
real-estate agent par excellence

Prologue

December 15

IT WAS SNOWING.

Again.

Claudia Claus just adored her hubby, and even after all their years of marriage, and even with his ever-growing love handles, just the tickle of his white whiskers against her face still sent shivers—and not those of cold—right down to her toes. And she loved their life together, but for some peculiar reason, this Christmas she had cabin fever in the *worst* way. The howling December wind, the blowing snow and deserted isolation of the North Pole were really getting to her. She'd had enough of the ice, snow, blizzards and subzero temperatures, and being ignored by Santa while he obsessively prepared for his annual gift run. Jeez, you would have thought that he could practically do it in his sleep. But, no. He was as nervous and persnickety as if this was the first time he'd taken the sled and reindeers out.

What she needed was a distraction—a little Christmas project of her own. Why, Santa probably wouldn't even miss her, he was so busy breathing down the necks of the elves, if she did take a small vacation. Last night when she'd breathed on his neck, hoping to lure him into the bedroom, he'd had the audacity to suggest that she might be out of shape!

She walked around aimlessly from room to room. Then, recalling Santa's crack, she searched for an aerobics tape and tried working out with Claudia Schiffer for a while. That didn't hold her attention for long. It was too discouraging. No amount of prancing and dancing was ever going to make her thighs as firm as Claudia's. For that, she'd require the magic of David Copperfield.

Ejecting the tape, she picked up one of the glossy women's magazines she'd taken to reading. She sat down in a wing chair in the bedroom, her attention riveted by an article encouraging women to do their own things. Escape convention. Shape their own lives.

It was just the encouragement she needed to rationalize her escape from frostbite temperatures and frigid boredom. And to keep her out of the Christmas cookies!

She went to pull her dusty suitcase from beneath the giant four-timber bed. A mischievous smile played at her lips as she planned her trip south. True, St. Louis wasn't that far south, but somehow she knew it wouldn't be wise to come back to the North Pole with a tan.

As it was, she was going to have to bring one heck of an extraspecial souvenir for Santa as a peace offering.

1

EVERY YEAR Hollie Winslow put up her Christmas tree at Thanksgiving, and every year her friend Sarah Smith came over on Valentine's Day to make her take it down. Hollie knew Sarah considered her a holiday freak, but Hollie didn't agree. She didn't think you could overdo such a bright, magical season.

The strings of colorful Christmas lights in combination with the dusting of snow on the cupolas and gables and cornices of the turn-of-the-century houses on Wisteria Avenue made the street appear shimmering with Christmas magic and spirit, Hollie thought as she drove along it. She was en route to the Premiere Homes real estate office for her last turn at manning the telephones before she began her annual vacation.

Suddenly she slammed on the brakes. The Victorian gingerbread house she'd had her eye on had a sign outside. She'd tried to list the vacant house herself, but had been unable to locate the owner. Darn! It now appeared another real estate agent had beaten her to the listing.

Curious about which agent had gotten the jump on her, she backed up her four-door sedan and pulled over to park in front of the house, skidding to a stop on a slick patch of road. Unsquinching her eyes after not hearing the crumple of fender, she breathed a sigh of relief at the sight of the still-intact red sports car jutting out of the driveway adjoining the house. By squinting just a bit, she could make out the sign posted in the long front yard.

It read:

Ms. Claudia
VISIONARY
Special Holiday Rates

Hmm . . . this was curiouser and curiouser.

Hollie decided to see who had rented the property and from whom. If it was on a short-term lease, maybe it would need to be listed after the holidays. She didn't want to work during the holidays anyway. The next ten days were carefully planned, filled with enough activities to make Martha Stewart look like a slacker!

She made the trip up the walk in her snow boots without event. On the front porch, she pressed the bell, expecting someone in gold hoop earrings and a fringed shawl to answer the door. Instead she was met by a stylishly white-haired woman wearing a red holiday sweater and green leggings.

"Come in, come in," the woman said, as if she'd been expecting Hollie. "I'm Ms. Claudia."

"Hollie Winslow," she replied, shaking Ms. Claudia's hand and smiling as she read the slogan on the woman's red top: "You ain't seen cute till you've seen St. Louis." Hollie recognized the whimsical artwork of a local artist, who was gaining a good measure of national fame.

"Would you like me to do a reading? The special holiday rate is only fifty dollars."

"Uh..." Hollie glanced down at her favorite yuletide watch with the Christmas tree on its face. "I don't have much time before I have to be at my real estate office."

"Well, we could do a minireading for, say, twenty-five dollars. I'll just hit the high points."

"High points?"

Ms. Claudia's laugh was merry. "You know, like what Santa's bringing you for Christmas if you've been a good girl. And of course you've always been a good girl."

Ms. Claudia had that much right. Orphaned at seven when her parents had been killed in an automobile accident, she'd first been placed in a series of orphanages, then had grown up in foster care when she wasn't adopted. Trying to please and be good hadn't gotten her love, but it had gotten her by. In foster care they hadn't wanted her to get used to any family, so they'd changed families every couple of years. Foster care was meant to be temporary care.

All that uprooting and loneliness had made her hunger for a home of her own. And she supposed it was the reason she had chosen to become a real estate agent—it was her way of finding just the right houses to become homes for her clients. And she found it immensely rewarding when she succeeded. She smiled to herself.

Since childhood she'd had this fanciful affinity for houses. They were as real to her as people. And each time she'd leave a house she'd say goodbye.

She looked around the hallway, taken by the oak staircase and paneling and the whimsy of the decoration. Something about this house was calling out to her. Hollie supposed it would be rude not to let Ms. Claudia do her reading—especially if she wanted to see more of the gingerbread house and to learn the name of the owner.

"The abbreviated reading would be all right, I guess."

Ms. Claudia nodded and took Hollie's red swing coat. After hanging it up on the brass coat tree, she led Hollie into the parlor, which was dominated by a huge, gloriously splendid Christmas tree, hung with balls, lights and Victorian-style ornaments. Perhaps Ms. Claudia had inherited the house. The place did suit her; both were cozy, familiar and inviting, Hollie thought, as she sat down in one of the green velvet wing chairs facing the blazing fire in the hearth.

"Now, what would you like to know?" Ms. Claudia asked, settling into the chair across from her.

"Who the owner of this house is," Hollie said with a smile.

Ms. Claudia laughed. "That's right, you're in real estate. Well, it isn't me. I've just leased it for the holidays. I answered an ad in the newspaper. Before you leave, I'll look up the number. I understand someone inherited the house, who isn't scheduled to take possession until after the holidays."

Hollie slumped at the news. It was such a darling house and she would have loved showing it. Oh, well, it wasn't meant to be.

"Surely there must be something else you want to know," Ms. Claudia said.

Hollie brightened. "Okay, what *is* Santa bringing me for Christmas?"

"Santa's got a great big package for you this year."

"How big?"

"Six feet one inch."

"What?"

"Santa's not bringing you a great big package with a bow on it—he's bringing you a beau." Ms. Claudia settled back in her wing chair, obviously delighted with her news.

"Wait a minute. Are you trying to tell me I should expect to find a man under my tree Christmas morning?" Hollie asked, laughing nervously.

"That's what I'm telling you. Anything else you'd like to know?"

"But...but there's not a man on my Christmas wish list. I wanted a bread maker—you know, one of those cool bread-and-butter makers." It really was what she wanted and she felt compelled to explain. "I sampled the bread from one of them in a housewares store a few weeks back. It smelled and tasted so-o-o good."

Ms. Claudia's eyes twinkled as she insisted, "So can a man."

Hollie felt herself blush. And she knew Ms. Claudia could tell. It was the fate of having a pale complexion—she lit up like a Christmas tree when she blushed.

"Are you sure about this? I'm not certain I want—I mean, I'm not ready for..."

"Love? How can anyone not be ready for love?" Ms. Claudia asked, sounding amazed.

"It's not that I'm not ready for love. I'd like to fall in love, but with the right man."

"And you haven't had much luck with men?" Ms. Claudia guessed.

"They tend to disappoint me."

"This one won't."

"That's what I tell myself every time. Oh, well, at least I'll get my holidays in before he shows up to disrupt my life on Christmas Day."

"You know, Hollie, peace and quiet can be way overrated."

"So can men," Hollie grumbled a few hours later as she neared the end of her shift at the real estate office. In only five minutes she'd be off on vacation and could begin enjoying the holiday season she adored. Thank goodness the real estate business was slow at this time of year and she had a lenient boss. She glanced down at her watch. In mere minutes she'd be out of here, and she began to gather her purse and things to leave. Then the phone rang.

"Premiere Homes," she answered, mouthing "go away" beneath her breath.

"I need an agent to help me—"

Hollie interrupted the client before he got too involved. Through the front window, she caught sight of Sandy Martin, the receptionist, who was just pulling into the parking lot. If she could hold this guy off, Sandy could take a message.

"If you'll just wait, I'll have the receptionist make an appointment for you—"

"No, that won't do. You don't understand. I need an agent right now. I've found a house I want to see today."

"But—"

He was better at getting his way than she was. "I need to find a house by Christmas. I've just transferred in from another town," he said, his deep voice firm and insistent.

She found herself weakening, despite her vacation plans. Of course anyone would want his family settled for the holidays. No man would want his family to spend Christmas in a motel.

He pushed his case.

"Look, I'll make it easy on you," he said, softening his voice. "I'll waive all rights to any inspection—and I'll pay cash."

A cash buyer was an agent's dream, and waiving all rights to an inspection was the icing on the cake. Only a fool would pass on a lucrative client with such potential. And a woman whose old car was having such an intimate relationship with the repair garage would have to be plain nuts. With the down payment for a new car dancing in her head, she felt herself caving in.

"Where is the house you want to see? Do you have an address for me?"

"Yes," he replied. "I stopped and jotted it down when I saw the For Sale sign in the yard."

He gave her the address and she logged on to the computer to look up the specs on the house in the MLS network of listings. She found the place easily enough. It was listed at three hundred thousand dollars, making her commission—if she closed the sale—nine thousand dollars!

"What time would you be available to look at it if I can schedule an appointment?" Hollie asked, trying to sound casual.

"As soon as possible. I want to buy a place by Christmas," he stressed.

"Okay, let me call the agent and see if I can set up a time for us to go through it. It's difficult during the holidays, so don't get your hopes up. Give me your number and I'll phone you as soon as I can."

He gave her the name of his hotel and she repeated it to him. "And your name?" she inquired.

"Noel."

"Did you say 'Noel'?"

"Is there a problem?" he asked with an edge to his voice.

"No, no. It's just that it's Christmastime and your name is Noel and my name is Hollie, Hollie Winslow."

"I'll be waiting for your call, Ms. Winslow." He replied so briskly that she felt foolish for bringing up the Christmasy associations of their names. She put down the receiver. Oh, well, she didn't have to like the man to sell him a house, and he most certainly didn't have to like her to buy the house. So why did it matter to her what kind of impression she'd made on him?

IT HADN'T BEEN an auspicious start to her holiday vacation, Hollie thought that evening at Leo's Garage, where she had been waiting for the past hour to have a new muffler installed in her car. Her old one had fallen off her car in the middle of the street, in the middle of rush hour, and she'd driven to Leo's making more noise than a freight train. Sandy had paged her that a Mr. Noel Hawksley was at the real estate office demanding to see her, more than a tad upset she wasn't there, demanding to know why she hadn't called back with an appointment to show him the house he wanted to see. Demanding to know if Ms. Winslow was always so inefficient. No doubt all his demands had fallen within earshot of the agency's owner. Hollie made a mental note to phone the owner the next morning and explain that she'd spent the afternoon driving by available stock in Mr. Hawksley's price range so she'd have something to show him if she couldn't get ahold of the agent who'd listed the house he wanted to see. That so far, she'd been unsuccessful in reaching the agent. Then her damn muffler had fallen off.

Aggravated, Hollie finished writing out a check for the new muffler. At least there hadn't been any more urgent pages from the real estate office while she was impatiently pacing at the garage.

As she ripped off the check from her checkbook to hand to the mechanic, she glanced at her cellular phone, which was lying beside her purse on the counter. She hoped it was working. It hadn't rung once. It was so frustrating trying to reach an agent during the holidays.

She'd wanted to get together with her anxious client, but it didn't look as if that was going to happen until tomorrow.

She glanced down at her watch again. Her godchild, Elena, was four years old, but had the patience of a two-year-old. Elena's mother, Sarah, Hollie's best friend, wasn't going to appreciate Hollie being late for their annual cookie-baking marathon. Most likely, Sarah had already started baking.

Hollie remembered the white chocolate Sarah had asked her to pick up. She'd have to make a stop for that and be even later. If she wasn't waiting for the agent to call, she'd call Sarah.

"Ring, damn it," she muttered, glaring at the silent phone.

She hoped this wasn't a foreshadowing of how her holidays were going to go.

Her vacation wouldn't swing into full gear until she'd settled her new client and his family in a new home for the holidays. With any luck at all, in the morning they'd get in to see the house he'd called her about.

She smiled as she handed Matt, who was new at the garage, her check. "Tell Leo thanks for fitting me in."

"Uncle Leo said any time you had trouble to take care of you right away."

Hollie laughed. "That's because I'm financing his holiday cruise with the repairs to my old clunker."

"I think it's because of your great smile."

Hollie blushed and he turned to ring up her check.

A woman in a holiday sweater came in looking for someone to repair a flat tire. The sweater made Hollie remember Ms. Claudia's promise of a six-foot-one-inch beau for Christmas. Leo's nephew Matt had a nice butt and he was kinda tall.

"How tall are you?" she surprised him and herself by asking when he turned to hand her the receipt for the work on her car.

"How tall?" he repeated.

She nodded.

"About five foot eleven," he answered, picking up the ringing wall phone.

Well, that left out Matt. Growing two inches by Christmas day wasn't within the realm of possibility. Neither was, Hollie smiled to herself, getting a tall, dark and handsome beau for Christmas. But it didn't stop a girl from hoping, did it?

On the drive home from the garage, she slipped in Kenny G's holiday tape and felt her stress melt as fast as last night's snowfall while the soothing notes of "Silver Bells" filled the car.

The cellular phone that had been annoyingly quiet rang, breaking into a soaring tenor sax solo.

"Hello," Hollie said, expectant.

"Where are you? You're supposed to be here already," Sarah said, her annoyance coming in loud and clear.

"And you're supposed to be the real estate agent I've been calling. What's up, Sarah?"

"Elena's insisting that I stop baking cookies and French-braid her hair like Auntie Hollie's. Did you remember the white chocolate?"

"Yeah, yeah. Tell Elena to find a ribbon for her braid and take a chill pill till I get there."

"Which will be . . . ?"

"Tonight, definitely tonight."

"Hollie—"

"Okay, okay. Fifteen minutes. Unless six foot one inch shows, and then don't wait up."

"What?"

"I'll tell you about it when I get there."

"Whatever, just get here. No, Elena, you can't feed the dog chocolate chips. . . ."

Elena answered the door when Hollie arrived. At four Elena had a mind of her own, a creative fashion sense and an advanced interest in makeup and hairstyles. At the moment she was dressed in a denim empire dress, hiking boots and her big, soft brown teddy bear backpack. "You're late," she announced.

"Where are you going?" Hollie asked Elena as Sarah peeked around the kitchen doorway, flour dusted on her nose and her hair in a haphazard ponytail.

"She isn't going anywhere," Sarah said. "She just refuses to take her teddy bear backpack off. Even sleeps with it."

"Should stand her in good stead as a Girl Scout—always be prepared, you know."

"Yeah, right. I'm wrist deep in big boy brownies. You said you remembered the white chocolate. . . ."

"Got it." Hollie produced it. "And a new muffler—that's why I'm late. I swear every time I build up my fund for plastic surgery, I have to use it on my car."

"What's 'lastic surgery, Mom?" Elena wanted to know.

"Auntie Hollie wants bigger 'bumpies,'" Sarah explained, refusing as she had since she'd adopted Elena to shield her from any information.

"Me, too," Elena agreed.

Sarah just shook her head. "You know, Hollie, I'm sending her to live with you when she turns thirteen."

Unrepentant, Hollie replied, "Good, then I'll have a whole new wardrobe to borrow from."

"I don't know which of you is the bad influence." Sarah took the white chocolate and nodded for Hollie to follow her to the kitchen. "You can drizzle the melted white chocolate and butter over the brownies when they come out of the oven."

"What about my French braid?" Elena pleaded, her "licksticked" pink pout evidence she had already been into her mom's makeup.

"I'll just be a sec," Hollie promised, taking Elena's tugging hand.

"I'm setting a timer," Sarah called out after them.

Hollie waved her hand over her head. "Yeah, yeah."

"Do you want to hear the Christmas song I learned at day school?" Elena asked, climbing up on the chintz bench in front of Sarah's makeup table.

Without waiting for an answer, Elena launched into "Santa Claus Is Coming to Town," while Hollie braided her hair in a reverse French braid. By the time

Elena had finished her rendition Hollie had tied the pink ribbon in a bow to anchor the braid.

"Now, let's go help your mom with the cookies."

"Okay," Elena agreed, scampering ahead of her. "Mom said I could ice the angel cookies."

Hollie could smell the rich brownies baking in the oven as she watched Sarah expertly roll out an eighth-inch-thick circle of dough.

"Hand me the angel cookie cutter, Elena," Sarah instructed, then showed Elena how to use it.

While Elena was busy pressing the white plastic angel cookie cutter into the soft circle of yellow cookie dough, Hollie began giving Sarah the third degree about her love life. "So, are you getting a diamond for Christmas?"

"If I buy one for myself."

"What happened?"

"It didn't work out. He was great with Elena, but—"

"But you didn't need a man to get Elena and so you certainly don't need to marry one just for Elena, right?"

"Do you think I'm wrong, Hollie?"

"No. I think if you're happy, Elena's happy. You adopted her because you have a lot of love to give. When you find the guy you can both love, then you won't hesitate. There's no reason to settle. Besides, if I don't like the guy Santa leaves under my tree, I'll send him over to you."

"What guy? What are you talking about? Did I miss a meeting?" Sarah asked, trying to keep up with the conversation and bake at the same time. Sarah had been running her own catering business from home since she'd adopted Elena. It provided a good living and gave her time to enjoy Elena's years before she started school. She was thinking of expanding her business once the little girl was in grade one. On sleepless nights, Sarah worked on plans for her new venture.

"Well, Ms. Claudia said—promised, actually—that I was going to find a *beau* under my Christmas tree."

"And Ms. Claudia is...?"

"She's the psychic who's rented the Victorian gingerbread house I told you about. For a small fee she'll tell you what the near future holds. Maybe you should give her a try. She's something else." Hollie thought Sarah could use the bit of fun, at the very least.

"I think I'll pass. I already know what the near future holds—parties. I've got a party booked nearly every night from now until New Year's Day."

"That's what you get for being Martha Stewart's clone."

"Hey, no mocking my idol," Sarah warned with a teasing grin as she put cookies in the oven.

"Perky Martha exhausts me. Her so-called simple projects take more skills than I could muster in a lifetime of lessons. Still, I have been thinking of doing one of those gingerbread houses she claims are a piece of cake to make."

"A gingerbread house! Oh, Auntie Hollie, can I help you?" Elena said, jumping up and down beside Hollie.

"You sure can, sugarpie. I'm on vacation—well, sort of, if I can get rid of Noel."

"Who's Noel?" Sarah asked.

"A client. I've got to find a house for him and his family by Christmas. Hopefully he'll like the one I show him tomorrow, if I can get hold of the listing agent. He's a cash buyer who could make my Christmas very merry, as in a down payment for a new car."

"Can I spend the night when we make the ginger-bread house, Auntie Hollie?"

"Sure, sugarpie. Your mom can use a break while she gets ready to cater all the parties she has lined up. We'll rent *The Little Princess,* take bubble baths, do our toe-nails bright cherry red and eat cookies in bed."

"Can we go now?" Elena stopped jumping and wrapped her arms around Hollie.

"No, tonight we have to bake the cookies we're go-ing to eat in bed. You're icing the angel cookies, re-member," she said, looking down fondly at Elena, who nodded, her eyes bright with excitement. She stroked Elena's silky hair. Hollie wondered if she'd have a daughter someday. First, though, she would need a husband, since she was nowhere near as brave as Sarah to raise a daughter on her own. Growing up never hav-ing been part of a family, she didn't have the heart to deprive her own child of what she herself had been so painfully deprived of. Her longing to create a home and a traditional family life hadn't gone down well with the commitment-phobic men she dated. She was beginning to fear that the family man had gone the way of the dodo and dinosaur.

NOEL HAWKSLEY STARED at the phone that didn't ring in his hotel room.

Early in the morning he was going back to Premiere Homes and make sure Hollie Winslow got his message. The one the receptionist had apparently forgotten to give her. He wanted a deal closed on the house he'd seen as soon as possible. He'd taken vacation until the first of the year to get the house business settled. No way did he want to spend Christmas in the States. He could sum up his feelings about the holidays in two words—bah, humbug.

He began peeling off his clothes, then hung up his suit in the tiny closet. His designer suits fit him to perfection because they were custom-tailored and because he worked out regularly. While he was stuck here, he would have to find a local gym to join to work off stress and keep his body honed. He would be in great shape when he started his job in the new year.

He wasn't the sort of man who plumbed the depths of his soul. Better not to swim in those murky waters. Instead he focused on his career in business—it gave him an edge as well as an escape.

Talk about escape. Last Christmas he'd narrowly escaped Marcy, his overly possessive ex-fiancée, though it hadn't seemed like a good thing at the time.

Escape.

That was what he wanted to do right now, but he had to find a house first. He picked up the remote on the night table beside the king-size bed and clicked on the television.

At least Hollie Winslow appeared not to like the season any more than he did. That was some consolation, he thought, stretching out naked on the bed.

The last thing he wanted was some perky, happy-holiday lover.

Meanwhile, back at the North Pole...

CLAUDIA'S NOTE was irritatingly vague, Santa noted suspiciously. She hadn't said exactly where the spa she'd gone to was. His wife just hadn't been the same since she'd started working out to those videotapes and reading those women's magazines she subscribed to. *New Woman,* indeed.

Not that he was complaining. He thought Claudia looked awfully sexy in the elf tights she'd taken to wearing with her funky holiday sweaters. His ho-ho-ho's had definitely gotten a lot jollier.

Still, he'd be a lot happier if he knew where this spa was...and just where she'd hidden the Christmas cookies when she'd left.

2

December 17

NOEL HAWKSLEY PULLED his black Lexus sedan up in front of Premiere Homes. After his morning cup of coffee he'd decided to pay his visit to Ms. Winslow early before he missed her again.

He groaned as yet another Christmas song came on the radio. He turned off the ignition and the song a lot easier than he could his dislike of the season. Born on Christmas Day, he'd never received a separate birthday present as a kid. That had given him a head start on hating the day. And then he'd gone into retail—scouting out new locations and administratively orchestrating the openings of Bon Marché's national chain of upscale department stores. Everyone in retail eventually grew to dread the month of December. Overworked and stressed to the max, Noel found little joy by the end of the month and escaped every Christmas Eve to St. Bart in the Caribbean. Lots of shapely women in bikinis and white pristine beaches were his reward for not committing murder most jolly.

The one time he'd been inclined to change his mind about the holidays had been a disaster. A year ago, the woman he'd thought he was in love with had sealed his hatred for the season by breaking their engagement on Christmas Eve. He'd never forgiven Marcy for that.

He got out of the car and went inside the real estate office, determined to have his way.

"Noel Hawksley to see Ms. Winslow," he announced to Sandy, who looked up as she took a call.

"First door on your right," she mouthed, her hand covering the receiver.

Noel followed her direction, and found a lush brunette sitting at a cluttered desk, muttering as she searched through the pile of papers in front of her for something. "Elena, you little squirrel, if you've taken my telephone book to color in..."

As she continued muttering and searching, he took a moment to glance around her office before announcing his presence.

At the sight of the framed poster on her right, he laughed outright, alerting Hollie. It was a picture of the famous Hearst Castle—San Simeon—and pasted across it was the banner "Sold Fast."

The woman blushed and tried to cover her embarrassment with a quick, businesslike "Can I help you?"

He offered his hand. "Noel Hawksley. You *do* remember talking with me?"

"Of course. I was just trying to find your number to call you. I've had trouble reaching the listing agent, but she finally returned my message this morning, and I've set up an appointment. The sellers are out of town for the holidays, but we can get in to see the house any time you like by using the agent's key."

"I'm ready whenever you are," he informed her, eyeing the pile of flotsam on her desk, which included a bottle of red nail polish, men's deodorant—she must subscribe to the never-let-them-see-you-sweat school of selling houses—pens, a cellular phone and sundry papers.

She swept the whole pile into her briefcase and flashed him a smile. "I'm ready."

She led him to her car, and he read the spec sheet on the house as she drove, restraining himself with difficulty from commenting on her propensity for changing lanes frequently. Usually erratic lane switchers drove him up the wall, but today, all things considered, a woman in a hurry was right up his alley. The sooner they found him a house, the happier he'd be.

"Were you thinking of private or public schools?" she asked as she waited at a stoplight.

"I'm out of school," he answered dryly.

"No, I meant—oh, you don't have children, then."

"No children."

"I see. Well, the taxes on this house are midrange. The neighborhood has a good tax base, what with it being close to the Galleria. Your wife will love the shopping there. It's where I'm going to do my Christmas shopping."

"No wife," he said, in a deadpan tone.

"Oh. Well, then *you'll* like the shopping there."

"No, I won't."

"Oh, you're like most men and don't like to shop."

"It's not the shopping I mind. It's the time of year."

"Don't you like the holidays?" she asked, surprised.

"I loathe them." That appeared to shock her. It was as if he'd said he didn't believe in Santa Claus. Maybe he shouldn't be so hard on her. She seemed primed to do her holiday shopping—the back seat of her car was filled with rolls of gift wrapping, packages of bows and unwrapped gift boxes in every shape and size.

She would probably be astonished to learn he knew more about shopping than she did. It was his area of expertise. He knew just what configuration of merchandise would make a consumer turn loose her credit card. Knew what music would put her in the mood to spend a lot of cash. Knew what colors would induce her to linger in an area long enough to make a purchase.

And more than all the technology and science, he had something of even greater value to offer—his gut feelings about trends and the desires of the consumer mass. More than anything, that was what garnered him the high salary and the respectful attention of Bon Marché's money men.

But it wasn't money that drove or satisfied him. It was curiosity. He was always restless and easily bored.

"We're here," Hollie announced as they pulled up to a two-story house with a brick walkway that led to a wide front porch.

"So we are." He followed her up to the house. She walked slower than she drove, but that could be due to the ankle-length, black wool gabardine skirt with a back zip and kick pleat that she was wearing. Her trim ankles were hobbled in suede boots with two-inch heels. Her short black suede jacket covered the rest of her, hiding the more interesting details of her anatomy.

The house was decorated with only a simple wreath at the door, Noel noted, as Hollie rummaged about in her briefcase to get the key to the front door. Like many businesswomen he knew, Hollie evidently used her briefcase as her purse to avoid having to carry both.

"Elena, I'm going to throttle you," she muttered.

"Is there a problem?" he asked as she grew more flustered, dropping to one knee for a closer look in her briefcase.

"I can't find the key. I'm sure it's in here somewhere. It has to be in here someplace. I'll have to pay a huge fine to replace it if it isn't. Please be in here," she begged, finally upending the briefcase in frustration.

"Sold Fast"? He couldn't imagine how. Ms. Winslow was about as professional and organized as a four-year-old.

He tried not to tap his foot as she sifted through the contents of her briefcase. He was certain the key wasn't there. This didn't bode well for seeing the house and making a buy anytime soon.

"It's not here," she finally announced.

To the surprise of no one.

"Now what?" he asked, truly curious, as he watched her scoop up her stuff and toss it all back into the briefcase, about how she'd handle the situation.

"Ah, I really hate that we made the trip for nothing."

She shoved her cloud of hair back and thought for a moment, while he waited, using the time to take in her lively green eyes.

"Okay, okay. I know, we can have a look in the windows since we're here." She walked over to the one on her left. The traditional-style house had tieback curtains, so one could easily see in through the multipaned glass.

She was actually serious, he realized, when she began describing the interior of the room, trying to sell him on the house from the outside.

"See, the dining room has a fireplace. That's a nice bonus, don't you think? It would be great for business dinners."

He came to stand beside her and glanced in, then looked down at her. "I don't have business dinners at home. I'm single, so I entertain in restaurants. I understand St. Louis has many fine such establishments."

"That's true. St. Louis is known for its Italian cuisine in particular."

Not giving up on her harebrained idea, Hollie moved to the window on her right. "Look, the living room has a fireplace, too."

She wasn't deterred when he didn't follow her to the window, just went on with her spiel about the room's selling points.

"Look at the big old rafters, and the pine floors are made of real tongue-and-groove boards. The French doors even have transoms."

"I'm more interested in whether the kitchen has a built-in microwave and whether the family room is large enough to accommodate a big-screen TV and a regulation-size pool table. You know—is the place livable?"

"A pool table," she repeated, clearly taken aback.

Obviously she didn't think he was the type. His cus-tom-tailored suit didn't suggest a taste for motorcycles and smoky rooms.

He shrugged. "Some people relax with yoga or fly-fishing. I play pool to get mellow."

"So let's see what's around back," she proposed. "This house has the typical St. Louis floor plan, with the living room and dining room side by side in the front of the house and the kitchen and family room in back, forming a perfect square box."

She was plucky; he'd give her that. And so, having nothing better to do, he trailed after her to the back of the house to see what the windows there yielded. If they could see in them.

The large cedar deck that ran across the back of the house afforded them an easy view of the rear rooms. He let her climb the steps to the deck first, enjoying the scenery... and not of the expansive backyard, either.

"Oh, it's plenty spacious for your needs," she cried out happily upon seeing the open-plan kitchen-family room. "See, there's a built-in microwave in the center island and the kitchen even has white painted cabinets with glass fronts so you won't have to remember where you put the coffee when you wake up grouchy."

He pretty much knew that was a dig. But peering in-side, he had to admit the house met his requirements nicely.

"Okay, this is looking good, but what about the half story above? I'll need some room for a home office, with enough electricity for a fax, computer, copier and such." He glanced at the windows four feet above their heads, then back down at her. "I suppose I could boost you up so you could stand on my shoulders and tell me...."

Hollie stared down at her long, narrow skirt and boots and then looked up at him again. "Not a chance. You'll just have to use your imagination."

Her reply got a flashy grin from the grinch. Clearly he was already doing just that—lasciviously.

Hollie knew they had gotten off to a bad start, with him thinking she was some incompetent fluff. But she knew better. And she was the one who would be smiling when she got the commission for selling him a house. Because she would sell it; she was very good at what she did.

As good as he figured he was.

HOLLIE'S RUSE of selling Noel the house from the outside hadn't worked. She couldn't believe she'd actually tried such a scheme. Every once in a while her Lucy Ricardo streak surfaced, despite her best efforts to keep it in check. And usually when she was confronted by someone stuffy like her tall broad-shouldered client. Noel Hawksley had perfect manners, and a peculiar effect on her. She was unaccountably nervous and self-conscious—as if they were on a first date instead of a first peek at a house.

She realized that her efforts to get inside were not just professionally motivated. She wanted him to like her. Why? She wasn't even sure she liked him herself. One thing for sure—it appeared no one ever played fast with rules around him. *Play* wasn't a word she'd bet was in his vocabulary. He was all business and that was just fine with her, she thought, sitting across from him in her office, where they'd returned so she could do a computer search and printout of other similar-style and -size houses in the area for Noel to examine if he didn't like the inside of the house he'd first sighted.

"Did I hear you say 'rats'?" he asked.

She looked away from the screen. "No room for an office for you in that one."

She sighed and wished she were at home making pomanders, creating the fragrance of Christmas for her house. Instead she'd let her excitement at the possibility of earning a big commission—and doing a good deed for a family in dire need, or so she assumed wrongly, of a home for Christmas—interfere with her holiday preparations.

Not only had Noel Hawksley turned out to be single, he was a grinch. She just knew he was going to be one of those clients who took a tremendous amount of time to find that elusive something he wanted to make the purchase, despite his claim he had to be moved into a house by Christmas.

"Maybe your blood sugar is dropping and making you testy. Why don't I buy you lunch? Then we can swing by Elena's—whoever she is—house to check on the key and spend the rest of the afternoon looking at houses."

"Elena is my godchild. Her mother is my best friend, Sarah. But you're right about lunch." Hollie switched off her computer. She'd only breakfasted on an angel cookie she'd filched last night from Sarah with a conspiratorial wink to Elena.

"Okay, I'll let you buy me lunch, since you insist. But first I need to make a quick call to Sarah to make sure she'll be home."

As it happened, they went to Sarah's first because Elena had a dance class scheduled.

When Hollie rang the bell, she heard the patter of little tap shoes and a childlike "I'll get it, Mommy." Hollie quickly prayed that Elena didn't blurt out anything terribly embarrassing. Hollie wasn't at all sure about Sarah's permissive child-rearing practices.

The door eased open and Elena launched herself into Hollie's arms. "Can I spend the night with you, Auntie Hollie? Can I, huh?"

"Uh . . ."

"Who's he? Is he your new boyfriend?"

"Sorry," Sarah apologized.

She got to the door just as Hollie felt herself turning red.

"Elena's wound up tighter than a top because of the holidays. She takes after Hollie, I'm afraid. Elena get down. You've got tap shoes on and you'll ruin Hollie's pretty suit."

Elena unwound her arms from around Hollie's neck and stretched them out to Noel, wriggling her fingers for him to take her.

Noel stepped back out of Elena's reach.

"Come on, sugarpie," Hollie said, setting the child down and taking her hand. "Let's go look for my key and telephone book you borrowed from me last night. Do you remember where you stashed them?''

"Sarah Smith,'' Sarah said, holding out her hand and shaking her head. "You'll have to forgive Hollie. She's a bit of a free spirit.''

"I've noticed. It's good, though, that Elena has a playmate.''

"Why don't you come out to the kitchen? I hear the dog scratching at the kitchen door to come in.''

Noel followed, leery about what might lurk in the topsy-turvy house. They passed a dining room table stacked high with enough Tupperware containers to start a franchise.

"I've been baking,'' Sarah explained. "Since adopting Elena, I've been catering from my home, and this year the orders for Christmas cookies have been huge. No one seems to have time to bake anymore, thank goodness.''

Sarah's kitchen was as welcoming as she was. The white glass-front cabinets were filled with cheery Fiestaware, and a jumble of pots and pans danced on a rack above the center island.

Sarah opened the kitchen door as Noel took a seat at the round table by the bay window. A froufrou black-and-white dog jumped into Noel's lap and put its little paws on his chest while it stood to lick his face.

"Midnight, get down,'' Sarah commanded.

Midnight was evidently hard-of-hearing.

"You aren't afraid of dogs, are you?'' Sarah asked, taking the animal and giving it a biscuit to distract it after she shooed it off Noel's lap.

"No. I'm just not used to them."

"That's a shame. It must be hard moving around a lot the way you do for your career."

So Sarah and Hollie had discussed him. Interesting.

"I like it. I like a challenge."

"Then Hollie's the right woman for you. Although men always have a way of disappointing Hollie. Oops, I shouldn't have said that," Sarah said, caught up in her matchmaking.

Before Noel could ask why men disappointed Hollie, the subject of their conversation came into the kitchen, victorious in her search for her phone book.

"Found it in Elena's backpack. I had to trade her a tube of your magenta lipstick for it, Sarah. Alas, no key."

"You didn't let her put the lipstick on—" Sarah was headed for the bedroom before Hollie could tell her that she was only teasing and the tube she'd traded was jelly-bean pink.

"So what do you think?" Hollie asked, taking the chair across from Noel.

"Think?" he repeated, a puzzled expression on his face.

"About Sarah..." she coaxed.

"She's nice—"

"Nice. She's fabulous. Great legs, big blue eyes, and she's a great cook and a wonderful mother."

"I thought we were looking for a *house* for me."

"Of course. But you're single, and I thought that maybe you'd..."

"Make a great father for Elena?"

"That wasn't my first thought after you backed away from holding her."

"I don't know what to do with little kids," he dodged.

"Then you're wrong for Sarah. She wants to adopt another one."

"Do you always do drive-by matchmaking?" he asked, rubbing the wood-grained top of the table with his long fingers.

"Much to Sarah's chagrin. Sarah thinks it's just fine to raise children without a father. I'm not so sure. What do you think?"

"I spent my childhood at boarding school. Only saw my father at holidays."

"How awful."

"Is it?"

"You don't think so?" Hollie was astonished at his matter-of-fact acceptance of a lonely childhood.

She'd always missed having parents; he'd had them and apparently hadn't enjoyed the bond she'd assumed every child would crave.

"Are you close to your parents now?" she asked, pushing.

"At holidays—except Christmas. That I don't celebrate anywhere but on a warm island away from all the madness."

"How can you not love Christmas?" She was serious. "It's the most magical time of the year. Anything can happen. Anything at all."

Midnight, done with her biscuit, jumped up into Hollie's lap, and she absentmindedly patted the animal's back.

"You're absolutely right."

He didn't seem to want to discuss it. "What time does your tree say?" Noel asked.

He nodded at her Christmas watch, which he obviously disapproved of.

"Definitely time for lunch. You have anything we can grab a bite of while I keep looking for the key?" Hollie asked Sarah as she joined them.

"Sorry, since Elena wouldn't take off the lipstick we had to find something that would match jelly-bean pink. How do peanut-butter-and-jelly sandwiches sound?"

"Like you've been around a four-year-old too long," Hollie said, wrinkling her nose. "Don't you have any grown-up food?"

"How about grilled cheese?"

"Perfect. I'll help. You don't mind grabbing a bite here, do you, Noel? It will give us more time to look at houses."

Noel shrugged, outnumbered and outmaneuvered.

Just when the kitchen was starting to smell buttery good, Elena wandered back in with a tape of *Cinderella* in her hand.

"Mommy, I can't reach the VCR. Will you put it in for me so I can watch like you said until it's time for dance class?"

Sarah was washing lettuce for a salad and Hollie was keeping an eye on the grilled cheese sandwiches so they didn't burn. Both women turned to Noel.

"I can handle the VCR," he assured them, and got up to give Elena a hand.

"You look like the handsome prince," they both heard Elena say as he followed her from the kitchen. The two friends broke up.

"Do you realize a four-year-old has better dating skills than either of us?" Hollie said.

"Yeah, I'm going to have to lock her in her room until she turns thirty. That's why I'm thinking of adopting an older brother for her."

"What did you think of Noel?" Hollie whispered so they wouldn't be overheard discussing their guest.

"What kind of man doesn't like kids or dogs?" Sarah replied. "It's like he's afraid of them."

"He grew up in boarding schools, so I don't think he's ever been around either."

"That's sad."

"He is kinda sad, don't you think?" Hollie slid the cheese sandwich onto a warm plate and began grilling another while Sarah mixed the salad.

"He said he likes a challenge, so I told him you were the perfect woman for him."

Hollie dropped the spatula in her hand with a clatter. "You didn't!"

"I did. Serves you right for matchmaking. Don't think I didn't know what you were up to."

"But now he's going to think *I* want to jump his bones, Sarah."

"Don't you?"

"Bury them, more like it."

"Sell that to someone who'll buy it."

"I'm not interested." Hollie emphasized her point by shaking her head. "He's not my type."

Sarah laughed. "Yeah, too tall, too broad-shouldered, too good-looking."

"He doesn't smile much," Hollie insisted.

"He will if he hangs around you for very long. You are a caution, girl."

"I'm just going to sell him—oops—" Hollie caught the grilled cheese that almost slid from her spatula to the floor "—a house and that's all. And hopefully in record time so I can enjoy the holidays. With any luck at all we'll find something this afternoon, and Mr. Noel Hawksley, the grinch, will be history."

"Grinch?"

"He hates Christmas."

Sarah erupted into gales of laughter, just managing to blurt out that Hollie and Noel were meant for each other—perfect opposites.

"Be that way," Hollie sniffed, patting her riotous curls. "And here I was going to tell you how much I liked your new haircut."

"Do you? It's a gum cut." Sarah carried the bowl of salad to the table.

"Gum cut?" Hollie added the plate of fragrant cheese sandwiches she'd grilled to a golden brown.

"Your sugarpie crawled into my bed when she had a bad dream last night and somehow her bubble gum got into my hair. So voilà, short haircut. I have to admit it's a lot easier to take care of than long hair. I don't know why I didn't try it sooner, since I'm always so pressed for time now."

"It makes you look like Demi Moore in *Ghost*."

"Then I'm keeping it."

"Call the grinch and Elena while I get plates, napkins and some chips," Hollie said, not wanting to face Noel after Sarah's inept efforts at matchmaking. Hollie thought her own attempts had been at least semi-subtle.

Sugarpie hadn't helped by reminding her that Noel did indeed look like the handsome prince.

Even she didn't believe there was a fairy godmother in existence who could turn Noel into a fun date. Even if Sarah did insist Hollie was a princess, intent on always getting things her way.

She had a plan: find a home for Noel fast, find a car for herself with her tidy commission, end of story. No magic slippers; no fancy ball; no handsome, brooding prince.

Now, that was what she called a happy ending.

NOEL LOOKED DOWN at the little princess who'd climbed up on his lap when he'd settled on the sofa after inserting the *Cinderella* tape in the VCR.

She seemed really comfortable, cuddling against him as she watched the fairy tale.

To his surprise, he felt really comfortable, as well.

Next thing he knew he'd be believing in fairy tales.

And happy holidays.

And happy endings.

He'd have to guard against that.

He'd especially have to guard against the foxy real estate agent starring in his fantasies. What was it about Hollie Winslow that tripped his switches? It was more than the body that wouldn't quit and the mind that eschewed logic in favor of magic.

Meanwhile, back at the North Pole...

SANTA SAT BACK in the recliner with his red stockinged feet up on the footrest. His tummy was stacked with women's magazines. The ones he'd found in Claudia's bathroom. If he was lucky, he might find the spa his wife had gone off to featured in one of them. She might have circled the name, giving herself away.

He hadn't had any luck yet finding the Christmas cookies she'd hidden. He'd looked and looked, even searching in the elves' quarters. They claimed not to have seen them. The reindeer shed hadn't turned up any cookies, either. He'd probably just imagined the crumbs on Rudolph's nose. Claudia wouldn't have fed his chocolate crinkles to the reindeer because she was miffed at him for ignoring her, would she?

He turned the page of the magazine he was holding and reached for the remote control, searching for the hockey game as he settled for some nonfat crackers he'd unearthed in the kitchen pantry.

Bah, humbug.

3

December 18

"So WHAT HAPPENED to Mr. Smith?" Noel asked the following afternoon on their way to see the house he was interested in after Hollie had finally found the key in another purse of hers, not Elena's.

"There's no Mr. Smith. Never has been. Sarah adopted Elena as a single woman."

"And you think Elena needs a father? She seems happy, if not a little spoiled, to me."

"Having grown up in orphanages and foster homes, I guess I will always think having two parents is the way it should be."

"How'd you happen to grow up in orphanages?" Noel's voice changed to a shout. "Look out, that cigar-chomping idiot in the big boat is drifting over into our lane."

Hollie maneuvered to avoid the bald-headed driver she'd seen without Noel's back-seat driving. "My parents were killed in an accident when I was little."

"And you weren't adopted? I find that hard to believe, with your cute curls and all. You must have been more trouble than you were cute."

"I could never seem to remember when visiting day was," she hedged. "When prospective parents came to look us over, I was always missing somehow."

"More likely you'd shinnied up a neighborhood fruit tree to steal peaches while everyone was occupied, then sold the peaches to the other kids later."

Hollie laughed. "How'd you know?"

"I'm in sales."

"So how did you happen to grow up in boarding school?" she asked, as they drove down the street the house was located on.

"My father was ambassador to Holland. He fell in love with a Dutch girl. They traveled around quite a bit so I was sent to boarding school in The Hague."

"That explains the slight accent."

"Yeah," he agreed. "Come on, Ms. Winslow, let's find out if you can sell me this house from the inside," Noel said, seeing he wasn't going to get a rise out of her.

A breeze lifted the bow on the holiday wreath on the door as Hollie inserted her key to get them inside the house.

"Sign in." Hollie slid the guest register on the table to him and handed him a pen.

Since she hadn't toured the house previously, they toured the place together. It had been professionally decorated, so it showed well. But the personal touches that give a house warmth were lacking. Anyone at all might have lived there. Hollie felt sad for the house. No pictures of loved ones anywhere. No children's drawings or funny cartoons or silly magnets on the refrigerator door in the kitchen.

With the exception of the clothes in the closets, the house looked as if it were a display home in one of the new developments nearby.

"What do you think?" Hollie asked when they descended the stairs from the second floor.

"You're the saleslady—you tell me. Why should I buy this house?"

"It's in a good neighborhood, the price is reasonable, it's low maintenance and you can move in before Christmas," she said, checking the sheet in her hand about the availability to make sure.

"But—"

"But?"

"I hear a but in your voice. Tell me why I shouldn't buy this house."

Hollie strolled to the expanse of windows in the kitchen and looked out over the large yard. The refrigerator kicked on and hummed in the silence between them. Finally she answered. "I don't think this is the right house for you." There, it was out—and she was certifiable. She was supposed to be selling him the house, not trying to discourage him from buying it. "This house is sad and deserves a happy family."

"What?" He looked at her, incredulous.

"Hey, I don't like it any more than you do, but you asked me, so I have to tell you. I don't think you and this house are a good match, no matter how much I'd like to sell it to you and get on with my vacation."

"That's your only reason—this feeling you have about me and the house?"

She nodded.

"Then let's write up an offer," he insisted, going to sit down at the kitchen counter, where she'd left her briefcase. "You did remember to bring an offer form?"

"Of course."

She joined him at the counter and withdrew the necessary form from her briefcase.

"What do you want to offer on it?" she asked after filling out the standard information on the form.

"Let's make it twenty thousand under the asking price."

She didn't say anything as she jotted down the figure.

"You don't agree?" he asked.

"It's your money. I'm just surprised you're haggling when you're so anxious to get into a house and out of town before Christmas."

"No one expects you to offer the full price. I may be anxious, but I'm not foolish. Or sad," he insisted.

Hollie laughed. "You don't like being told anything, do you?"

"And you do?" he countered, signing the offer she slid across the counter to him.

He had her there. She didn't like being told much. Growing up alone had made her self-sufficient.

"Well, I'll present the offer for you and let you know as soon as I hear something." She folded the form and put it in her briefcase, then withdrew the cellular phone. "As soon as I put in a call on it, we can go."

Noel didn't walk around and inspect the house further while she made the call. He couldn't have appeared more uninterested. The house must just be a business investment for him, she decided. He'd probably grown tired of living out of hotel rooms. Sarah had mentioned something about him moving every year to set up new stores. What a terribly lonely life. No wonder he was sad.

She felt sorry for both him and the house.

HOLLIE HADN'T BELIEVED Noel was serious when he volunteered to go shopping with her while they waited to hear back on his offer. She had thought he'd be a wet blanket, complain nonstop about how long it took her to make up her mind, the holiday crowds, the long waits.

Instead he'd been a lot of help. With his assistance, she'd already gotten her business gifts out of the way, negotiated a great deal on some new lights for her Christmas mantel and found the Barbie Elena wanted for Christmas.

The last Barbie like it in the toy store.

Unfortunately, the Barbie had on the wrong color dress. Elena wanted the one with the pink dress, not the peach one. Noel even understood the distinction. She stood pondering the dilemma in the middle of the crowded toy store, her arms full of packages. He'd offered to carry, but she hadn't wanted to push her luck. The smart thing would be to return to the car and unload the packages into the trunk.

However, she didn't want to buy the Barbie in the peach dress if the toy store at the other end of the mall had it in the pink dress. She knew that if she put down the Barbie she'd found, the chances were very good someone else would buy it before she returned to the store. Better a Barbie with the wrong color dress than no Barbie at all.

"Here, you hold this," Hollie said impulsively, shoving her packages and the Barbie into Noel's arms. Left with two small Barbie accessory packets, she slipped them into Noel's jacket pocket. "Whatever you do, hang on to the Barbie. I'll be right back."

"Where are you—" Noel started to ask, but she'd disappeared into the crowd.

The only thing he could do was wait—not his favorite thing.

And worse, clutching a Barbie the woman with the red hair was eyeing.

A four-year-old miniature of the woman was tugging her arm, yelling, "I want that Barbie, Mommy. I want it—I want it."

"There aren't any more," the woman tried saying patiently.

"But I want it," the child screamed.

Tired and cranky and just full of the holiday spirit, Noel thought, wanting to be somewhere else. He glanced around for Hollie, but she was nowhere in sight. If he moved she'd never find him, so he was stuck.

"I want that Barbie, Mommy. Why does that man have a Barbie?"

Oh, great. Now he felt like a pervert. And people were beginning to stare.

The woman approached him with her child in tow. "Are you planning to buy that doll?" she asked.

"Maybe," he answered honestly.

"Well, when will you know? Because if you don't plan to buy it, my daughter wants it."

"I'm waiting for someone," Noel explained lamely.

"Can I hold it?" the little girl asked, her tears making her eyes bright.

He knew better, but he was on the spot. Besides, what could it hurt to let the little girl hold the doll? Once her fascination was done with, she'd move on to wanting something else. Even children lost interest in things they'd wanted desperately, once they had them.

He relented and handed the doll to the little girl, who presented him with a smile. Noel wished Hollie would hurry up and return.

Another younger woman, perhaps twenty, felt the material of his jacket, distracting him.

"Where did you get your jacket? I need a present for my boyfriend and I really like yours. Was it terribly expensive?"

"It's ah..." Noel couldn't remember who the designer was.

"Can I check the label . . . ?" the bold young woman asked, inching closer, reaching upward with her arm.

"It's Calvin Klein," Noel blurted, backing away.

He was getting warm, and the din of the shoppers was closing in on him.

Where was Hollie?

The young woman was incorrigible. And it was clear now that more than the jacket interested her.

"Was that doll you were looking at for your little girl?" she asked.

It was plain to Noel she meant "Are you married?"

"No. It's for—" He glanced around and his stomach sank. The little girl and her mother were gone.

And so was the Barbie.

"Excuse me," he said, moving away from the woman flirting with him to search for the two who'd lifted the Barbie he was supposed to be holding for safekeeping. He didn't want to be there when Hollie got back if he'd lost the doll.

But the two weren't in the front of the store by the register. They'd checked out in record time, and now he'd never find them. Well, there was no use in waiting around in the store for Hollie to appear. He might as well find her and tell her he'd screwed up and get it over with.

He thought he'd heard Hollie mutter something about another toy store when she'd left. He asked the checkout clerk, who said there was one at the south entrance. Just as he was exiting the store to find it, loud beeping went off.

"Sir, sir. You have to wait," a young male clerk yelled after him.

While Noel stood where he was, the clerk called the manager to come to the front of the store. The manager still had pimples, and he had an attitude about having responsibility. He had something to prove to Noel.

"If you'll just step back inside the store and come with me," he instructed Noel.

"There's some mistake," Noel stated between clenched teeth.

"If you'll just come back to my office."

Everyone had stopped to stare, making Noel feel like a criminal. He knew he hadn't stolen anything, but no one else did.

Hollie chose just that moment to return.

"Hey, John, how's the new house?" She'd met John Pritchard a couple of months earlier when she'd helped him and his young wife find the ideal starter house—a cozy two-bedroom in the suburbs.

"Great. We love it. On another matter, do you know this man, Hollie?" John asked.

"Yeah, he's shopping with me. Why?"

"The beepers went off when he tried to leave the store."

"What? Are you trying to steal the Barbie, Noel?" Hollie teased.

"I don't even have the Barbie," Noel said, fuming.

"What?" The teasing note was gone from Hollie's voice. "What do you mean, you don't have the Barbie?"

"I let a little kid hold it and she took off with it," Noel explained.

"There you have it, John. Some little kid set off the beepers."

John glanced at the clerk by the door, who shook his head no.

"We'll need to look in your packages, sir," John insisted.

"Jo-ohn!" Hollie pleaded, embarrassed.

Noel could see the kid was determined, so he handed over the packages. He knew all about security systems and something had made this one go off. Unless it was malfunctioning. It didn't take much imagination to guess what had happened. Someone must have bumped something into one of his shopping bags. This could all be easily explained away as an accident if he just let the kid have his moment of glory.

John went through the shopping bags, while *everyone* looked on as though they were witnessing the climactic third act of a play. The moment was anticlimactic, however, because not a piece of merchandise from the store was in the shopping bags.

"See, I told you," Hollie stated triumphantly.

"We'll need you to empty your pockets," John said, ignoring Hollie.

"But, Jo-ohn!"

"It's store policy, Hollie."

So the system *had* malfunctioned. It was Noel's turn to be cocky. With an exasperated sigh, he reached into his pockets—and his face fell. Besides some change there *was* something in his left pocket. Reluctantly, he withdrew it for John to see.

"I don't know how these got here," Noel insisted, looking at the two small packets of Barbie accessories as if they were tiny alien spaceships that had somehow landed in his pocket.

"I do," Hollie interrupted.

"You do?" both John and Noel said.

"I put them there when I gave you everything in my hands to hold."

"Thanks for telling me."

"So this is really all an innocent misunderstanding," John said, taking the two packets. "You really didn't mean to, ah..."

"No, I can assure you I didn't mean to, ah..." Noel informed him. "Am I free to go?"

"Go," John said, handing the confiscated merchandise to the clerk. "And you, Hollie. Next time be sure you don't—"

"I will, John. Promise." She hurried out of the store after Noel, whose long legs were carrying him to the nearest exit.

"Will you wait up for me?" she said, finally catching up to Noel, struggling with her full shopping bags. "Can't you see the funny side to this?" she pleaded as they left the mall together.

He stopped and scowled down at her. "There is nothing funny about almost being arrested for shoplifting," he declared. "Nothing funny in the least."

"Come on, weren't you just a little excited about the possibility of handcuffs?" He looked sexy when he was angry. She liked making him lose his tight rein on his emotions.

"No."

"Yeah, I keep forgetting how stuffy you are," she said, as he picked up the shopping bags she'd set down and followed her to her car.

"*I am not stuffy.*" She made him nuts.

"Yeah, you're just a real picnic in the park." He made her nuts. "Okay, okay. Let's just say we're even."

"'Even'?" Clearly he didn't believe what he was hearing.

She unlocked the trunk of her car and he piled the shopping bags inside. "Even. I might have nearly gotten you arrested, but you let a little girl rip off my Barbie doll. Do you know how hard that doll is going to be to find? And Elena has her heart set on it."

"Well, I wasn't about to try to take the Barbie away from that little girl once she had it. Can you imagine the scene that would have caused?"

Hollie laughed as the two of them got into the car. "Man, you sure don't like to be embarrassed."

"I don't think anyone in his right mind wants to be handcuffed and carted off to jail. It's not my idea of a real good time." At least the "carted off to jail" part wasn't.

"Oh, lighten up, Noel. *I'm* going to have to be fin-gerprinted for my job if the news media have their way. Some dumb study found there are more felons in real estate than any other profession. Since we have access to people's homes..."

"Speaking of homes, your beeper didn't go off sig-naling we had a deal on my offer, did it?"

"I'd have told you." She exited the parking lot.

"Even in all the excitement?"

"I know you don't believe it, but I'm good at my job."

"So you sold John a house?"

"Yeah, the cutest little starter house when he got promoted to store manager."

They drove down Lindbergh through Kirkwood. Big red lanterns covered each streetlight and swags of greenery trailed down the poles.

Hollie loved it.

Noel just sulked, refusing to let Hollie cheer him up. Refusing to admit his attraction to Hollie.

But Hollie didn't need anyone to have fun. She could have fun all by herself. She had learned how to grow-ing up alone more or less.

She began singing Madonna's saucy version of "Santa Baby" as they headed for Garvey's Restaurant on Telegraph. Their special onion blossom appetizer and an ice-cold St. Louis brewery product would put Noel in a much better mood; she just knew it.

Noel sat across from her feeling like Wile E. Coyote having run off a cliff, his body still in free-fall. Hollie

Winslow could make him furious, laugh, shy—she could make him feel. She was a dangerous woman. The sooner he bought a house the better.

He'd only really just met her and he already knew.

He felt sexier all over.

He'd volunteered to go shopping with her.

He'd volunteer to do anything to be with her.

It was too fast. He didn't want it.

He wanted it desperately.

Most of all he didn't want to disappoint her.

Garvey's was a bistro cum sports bar. It was known for its delicious food, casual atmosphere, fifty-two-inch televisions you could see from every table and cold beer by the bucket at an economy price. Since two could eat a tasty meal for under twenty dollars, the place was always busy, even on a Wednesday night. Of course, Hollie being in real estate seven days a week, one day seemed much like any other.

When they were seated Hollie noticed *Miracle on 34th Street* was playing on every television screen. She grinned to herself, thinking how very much Noel would love to be able to escape the sentimental movie.

Hollie suggested she order since she knew the menu by heart, and Noel acquiesced. She ordered the onion blossom appetizer that Garvey's had built its reputation on. Unlike most fried onions, these weren't greasy. The batter was just sweet and crisp. The pretty young waitress brought them and two cold beers while they waited for their grilled chicken pastas.

"Are you sure your beeper's working?" Noel asked.

"It's working," she promised. "You've got to be patient. A lot of emotion is involved in letting go of a house, even if you've made the decision to sell. I've had people change their minds at the very last second."

"But you think I'll get the house?"

"I don't know. It hasn't been on the market that long. The probability is that they will at least counter your first offer."

"So this could drag out a while..."

"Yes. Try the onion blossom and quit worrying. That's my job. Have you seen this movie?" she couldn't resist asking as Noel bit into the fragrant onion petals and made approving noises. "I just love it."

"I've managed to avoid it so far." He glanced up at the screen, then away quickly, as if the Christmas spirit might be catching.

"So how come you want to buy a house instead of renting, or just living in a hotel while you're opening a new store here?" she asked. "Not that I'm trying to talk you out of buying."

"This might be my last store opening."

"Have you been fired? Are you about to be laid off? Should I run a credit check?"

"Nothing like that. I told you it was a cash sale. I'm getting bored and ready for a new challenge. The worldwide market of the Internet interests me."

Of course it did. He probably spoke more than one language. He'd had a European education. His background even showed in his appearance. His clothes had a European flair. He dressed very well. Better than most men. She'd chalked it up to his being in retail. But it was more than that. Noel Hawksley had style. She didn't want to think about how attractive he was. No self-respecting Christmas freak could find a grinch attractive. That would be nothing short of emotional suicide.

A tall young man approached their table and stopped.

"Hi, I'm Jake. Your waitress has been called away. Her mom's car wouldn't start. I'll be taking care of the rest of your order. Would you like anything else?"

Jake had a great smile, and was distracted by the movie momentarily. "Sorry, I just love this movie."

"How tall are you, Jake?" Hollie asked impulsively, looking for a path away from where her thoughts had been leading.

"Six-three. You're thinking I play basketball, aren't you? Well, you're right, and isn't it cool we're in the finals? Did you want my autograph?" he joked.

"Just our food," Noel interjected.

"Right, let me check on that."

"Why did you ask him how tall he was?"

"I was just curious, that's all," Hollie said evasively.

Moments later Jake returned with their pastas. He'd no sooner set them down than her beeper went off.

"It never fails. Cold food again," she said, checking the beeper. "Looks like we've got an answer. I'll make this phone call and be right back. You go ahead and eat before the food gets cold."

She returned a few minutes later with Noel's answer. "Sorry. You lost the house. Someone else came in with a bid at the same time closer to the asking price. The owner took their offer, of course."

Noel wasn't sure how to react to the news.

He should be disappointed, not oddly relieved because he found himself wanting to spend more time with Hollie.

He wasn't used to not getting his way.

And yet, somehow he knew this holiday was going to have its way with him.

Whether he liked it or not.

Meanwhile, back at the North Pole...

WELL, AT LEAST he was making the long-distance telephone companies have a Merry Christmas, Santa thought as he dialed yet another spa in the warmer climates. So far he hadn't had any luck tracking down Claudia.

"Hello, I'm trying to reach a Claudia Claus. Do you have anyone registered at your spa by that name?" He waited while the person at the other end of the line checked.

"No, I'm sorry, sir. We have no one registered by that name."

Santa hung up the phone glumly. What he was doing was useless anyway. Most likely Claudia had registered under an assumed name. If only he didn't miss her so much. This was the first time they'd ever been separated and it told him just how much he took her for granted. He hoped she was just teaching him a lesson and hadn't left for good.

To distract himself from that gloomy prospect, he put on his parka and trekked outside to the workshop. The elves were grumbling because he had them working overtime to make more Barbies in pink dresses.

It seemed every little girl in the world wanted one.

4

ON THE DRIVE over to her office to check out some more house listings on the computer so she could take Noel out looking again, Hollie passed the Victorian gingerbread. She stopped, backed up to pull into the driveway and parked. Perhaps this house would suit Noel. She'd left without getting the phone number Ms. Claudia had promised her.

She was about to ring the doorbell, when the door opened and two teenage girls came out. They were too busy comparing predictions to pay much attention to Hollie, who went on inside.

"Hello," she called out.

Ms. Claudia called back "Coming," and appeared a few moments later. "Why, hello—Hollie, isn't it?"

"Yes. I forgot to take the phone number from you for the owner of this house. I have a client who might be interested."

"Sure, let me just get it for you." She disappeared into one of the rooms and returned holding a card with the phone number written on it. "Here you are." She handed the card to Hollie. "How's your new beau?"

"You mean six foot one inch?" Hollie asked, tucking the card in her briefcase.

Ms. Claudia nodded.

"Haven't seen him. I think about the only way I'm going to find six foot one inch under my tree for Christmas is if I order in pizza Christmas morning and mug the delivery guy."

"I don't understand," Ms. Claudia said, looking puzzled. "I must have made some mistake in my calculations. He should have shown up by now."

"Not to worry. Maybe I'll get that bread-and-butter maker I was wanting. Well, I've got to run. Thanks for the phone number."

Outside, Hollie glanced down at her festive watch and saw that she did indeed have to hurry. She had agreed to meet Noel at the office and he freaked at tardiness. If she was going to spend the whole day with him looking at houses she didn't want him in a crabby mood.

At any rate, he was going to have to learn to lighten up.

With a quick peek in her rearview mirror, she backed out of the driveway.

And smack-dab into another car.

Now she was going to be late for sure and Noel would be furious. Her day had suddenly turned rotten.

When she checked her rearview mirror again and saw whose car she'd backed into, her day turned completely rotten.

Noel was already out of his luxury car, the back of his wrists resting on his lean hips as he surveyed the damaged grille, then watched her approach.

"Are you all right?" he asked, concern in his voice.

"Of cour—" She began blinking to fight off a sudden bout of light-headedness. When she saw the damage to his car she, too, felt sick to her stomach. Choosing the coward's way out, she gave in to the light-headedness.

His strong arms caught her on the way down.

"Hollie, Hollie..."

At the alarm in his voice, she blinked away the fuzzies and opened her eyes. "I'm fine. Put me down. I only had a bottled water for breakfast. My blood sugar must have plummeted for a few seconds." She glanced at his car again. "Oh, no, look at your car. Where did you come from? I checked my rearview mirror before I began backing out."

"Your mirror must have a blind spot—or you do. But forget about the cars for now. I want to know how you are."

"If you'll please put me down you'll see that I'm fine," she instructed. She was happy that he was more concerned with her than his car. She'd dated men who weren't.

He set her down and she didn't faint.

"I think both cars are drivable. It's just a fender bender. Why don't I follow you to your house and we can do the insurance stuff there? You'll be a darn sight more comfortable than here in the street, and a lot safer.''

It started snowing as Noel and Hollie pulled up in their damaged cars in front of her little white frame house. The front door was a bright cheery red, Noel noticed while appreciating the symmetry of the green shutters decorating the small wood-paned windows. As he got out of his car, the sound of a holiday banner being whipped around by the wind caught his ear. It was definitely getting colder.

''Here, take my arm,'' Noel offered, helping Hollie out of her car.

When they reached the front door, he took her keys from her and opened the door, then followed her inside.

The first thing that hit him was the smell of pine. Her Christmas tree was announcing it was already up and probably decorated to the nines.

Everything sparkled—windows, mirrors, glass bowls of fruit and candy, he saw, when they entered the living area of the house from the tiny foyer. The layout was open kitchen and a greatroom-dining room. The twelve-foot windows that looked out over the backyard gave them a view of the falling snow, almost bringing it inside.

Hollie shook off a chill. ''I think I'll light a fire.''

''Just tell me where the woodpile is,'' Noel said. ''I'll get the fire going.''

''I'm afraid to disappoint you, Daniel Boone, but all it takes is a flick of the wrist. The fireplace is gas, though it looks real. And the house doesn't get as dirty. Come see."

She was right. It did look real.

He helped her out of her red coat and she took both their coats to the hall closet. When she returned she was rotating her shoulders and moaning.

"I thought you said you were all right." He started to get up from the sofa by the fire.

"Just a little sore from the seat belt," she explained. "I'll get us some hot chocolate and cookies and we can call the insurance companies."

"Can I help?"

"No, just enjoy the fire."

Noel did just that while taking in his surroundings. Candles of all sizes in holders of all descriptions, including hollowed-out apples on the coffee table, were everywhere. A garland of pine was draped over the mantel, which was also decorated with holly and clumps of baby's breath. A loop of fat yellow yarn held the holiday cards she'd already received from friends.

He smiled, delighted—despite his aversion to Christmas—by the festive beauty and homey warmth of her decorations.

Noel stared into the fire. The flames hypnotized him, making him sleepy. He'd stayed up late watching a movie on pay TV in his rented room. As soon as he got this house business settled and had relaxed on a tropical island over the holidays, he'd be ready to start work on opening the new store. Since he threw himself into his work, he didn't quite know what to do with himself when he wasn't working.

It was probably why he was crowding Hollie about finding a house. He should feel guilty, since she was supposed to be on her vacation. Maybe they would find a house later. When the snow stopped. Right now he just wanted to sit by the fire and relax. It was very comfortable in Hollie's house.

"Here we are," Hollie announced, bringing in two mugs of hot chocolate, which she placed on the coffee table. "I put some butterscotch schnapps in the hot chocolate to calm our nerves—well, mine anyway. What do you think?" she called back over her shoulder as she went to get the cookies she'd warmed in the microwave.

"Pretty smooth. Listen," he said when she came back with a plate of assorted cookies, "do you have any board games we can play? I think we should wait till it stops snowing before we go look at houses."

She picked up a chocolate crinkle cookie and bit into it while she thought. "I've got a game of Monopoly. And, of course, Candyland, for when Elena stays over."

"Monopoly," he decided.

"Why don't you call your insurance company while I find the game?" she suggested after a sip of hot chocolate to wash down the cookie, and she handed him the portable phone.

He certainly looks comfortable, Hollie thought as she rummaged through a closet for the game. The accident hadn't caused him any ill effects. She was the one with a new bill to pay. Her insurance would total her car for any dent over three hundred dollars because that's all her car was worth. She'd be out a car or the money, since that was the amount of her deductible. Maybe she could just hang a wreath over the bumper until she sold Noel his house and got her commission. The car was still drivable; that much at least was good news.

She looked out the window of the bedroom Elena slept in when she stayed over. At least for part of the night. By morning Elena had usually finagled her way into Hollie's bed. It was still snowing. If it kept up she wasn't going to be able to track down that Barbie doll for Elena until tomorrow.

Her whole holiday was off kilter because of the man in her living room. And worse—she was off kilter. Noel Hawksley was a distracting man. He made her remember she was a woman. A sexual being.

She smiled as she picked up the game he wanted to play. Off kilter or not—she planned on winning that round with Noel.

She didn't win.

Noel played the game like Attila the Hun. Even knowing Noel's aggression was fueled by his need to be thought of in a certain light, Hollie wasn't a good loser. Not for the second time. He'd sent her straight to jail without passing go to collect her money one too many times.

"That's it. I don't want to play anymore," she announced when he gloated over his second win.

"But it's still snowing and I'm not playing Candyland," he said, and polished off the last cookie on the shiny red plate.

"I'm going to get some stuff done, like wrapping the presents I bought yesterday. Want to help?" she asked, knowing he wouldn't.

"I'm all thumbs," he insisted. "Mind if I take a nap here on the sofa by the fire until it stops snowing? You will wake me up when it does, won't you?"

"Sure, go ahead," she agreed as he toed off his loafers and—finally—loosened his tie. It didn't escape her notice that he was a perfect fit for her long sofa. She'd been torn between a love seat and a sofa, and had settled on the long, overstuffed sofa in yellow-and-navy chintz.

He didn't even look out of place on the chintz.

She decided not to notice and went to get her packages to wrap.

By the time Hollie had gathered up her packages, Noel was snoring softly in front of the fire. It was just as well he hadn't offered to help; he would have given her a lot of grief over how she wrapped her presents. Christmas brought her creativity to full bloom and every year she did something different in the way of wrapping.

This year she'd decided on white wrapping paper, which she tied with bright red yarn. Then, with the help of a glue gun, cotton, glitter, buttons and bows, she personalized each package with Santas and elves and reindeer, before using red marker pens to outline the recipient's name, which she then filled in with red glitter.

It wasn't an idea she expected ever to repeat because it was extremely time-consuming... over-the-top Martha Stewart. Still, when she had all the gifts personalized and stacked under the tree they did look awfully festive and special.

Noel had proved to be a deep sleeper. He hadn't moved once.

She watched him sleep and thought about her feelings for him. Instant annoyance had given way to a begrudging attraction of sorts. She could imagine him as the lonely boy at boarding school and forgive him much because of it. She'd had the same loneliness for a companion growing up. As she was making allowances for his broody behavior, his expression shifted. He moaned and a sexy smile crossed his lips.

She hoped he was dreaming of her. No, what was she thinking? She didn't want— Well, if she were smart she wouldn't allow her thoughts to linger over questions like how it would feel to have his lips linger over hers for real. Was he a good kisser? Would a kiss from him make her swoon? She wasn't the swooning sort, of course, but he was the tall, dark and handsome type who was likely given to making women swoon.

Lean and fit, he was probably a tireless lover.

Yes, but was he a selfish lover?

He didn't seem the type who was given to foreplay and sensitivity. He'd sweep her off her feet and have his way then leave. He wasn't the sort to fix breakfast in the morning as a show of tenderness.

Tender. Now that was funny. Noel was about as tender as a cheap cut of steak.

Just because he looked yummy when he was asleep didn't mean he was a dreamboat awake.

If she were the sort of woman who liked to make men over, who believed a man could change, then Noel might be a challenge. But she'd made enough bad choices to know that people seldom changed.

Noel was what he was. A grinch.

A sexy grinch, but a grinch nonetheless.

So any fancies she had about him—fancies about her being the woman who could tame him—were best left in her imagination. She could indulge herself with how it might feel to be kissed, caressed and more by the man asleep on her sofa, but to let down her guard and fall victim to Noel's charm was foolishness she couldn't afford.

He could bruise her heart, even break it.

Business.

That's what Noel was interested in. He wanted a house before Christmas. And it was what she had to remain focused on as well.

She would find Noel an irresistible house. She would close the deal and make both of them happy. He would have his house and she would have her new car and they both would have a Merry Christmas.

If Noel Hawksley was indeed capable of having a Merry Christmas.

She saw that now his eyes were moving beneath their lids. He was dreaming. Probably about killing Santa Claus, from the wicked smile that had shifted on his lips. She glanced to the window.

Rats. It was still snowing and business was going to have to wait despite her determination to get on with it. They weren't likely to see any more houses until tomorrow.

Deciding to make up her holiday Cherry Walnut bread for the neighbors, she went to the kitchen. Her refrigerator revealed she had all the necessary ingredients but eggs. Since there was a small market just two blocks away, she decided to walk over for the eggs while Noel slept peacefully.

She grabbed her red coat and headed out into the snowy afternoon. As she walked in the snow, her thoughts kept returning to the very complicated, the very sexy, the very exasperating man sleeping on her couch.

"YOU DO KNOW I'm planning to have my way with you, don't you?"

Noel decided he must be dreaming.

His real estate agent was behaving very unprofessionally. The look in her eyes was one of planned seduction. She twirled one of her sexy curls with her forefinger as she flirted with him. She had changed into a provocative outfit. The baby T-shirt clung to her soft breasts. He knew they'd bounce when she walked, because he'd seen them do just that. His agent, it seemed, didn't have the need or desire to wear a bra. The beige cotton drawstring pants were tied loosely, so they rode low to reveal a cute-as-a-button navel.

A navel he wanted to explore with his tongue.

"I'd be much obliged if you did just that," he heard himself say.

"Do you want to touch me?" she asked, remaining just out of range.

"Desperately." He reached for her, but she evaded his grasp.

"First the rules," she explained.

"Rules?"

"Uh-huh. I can touch you, but you can't touch me."

He thought a moment. It wasn't the best deal, but it was better than no touching at all. He lifted his hands in surrender. "Okay, you're the boss. I'm your playground."

"Why don't I trust you?" She studied him a moment, then ordered, "Put your hands behind your head."

"Done," he said, following her rules.

She knelt before him. "You're quite handsome, you know. Those clear blue eyes and dark lashes are a lethal combination."

"You're just trying to flatter me so you'll get what you want, just like all the girls."

"Lots of girls..."

"Legions," he bragged to annoy her.

"But none like me." She said it with such quiet confidence that he believed her. Believed her because when she stroked his cheeks, his eyes, his lips, her touch was gentle—a tender caress.

"No, none like you," he breathed.

She began unbuttoning his shirt. "I can feel your warm skin through the cloth. Am I making you hot, Noel?"

"Ah, could you hurry up a little..." he pleaded, just keeping himself from thrusting.

"Oh, no. We go slow, excruciatingly slow. I plan to make you suffer to get your reward. You aren't the only one who can play games, Mr. Hawksley."

"I think under the circumstances you should call me 'Noel.'"

"But you don't like your first name, do you, Noel?"

"It's not a proper name."

"I love it. Noel and Hollie—it's like we were meant to be together." She pushed back his shirt. "Umm, smooth warm skin and rock-hard muscle. Very impressive for a businessman, Noel. Where'd you get this washboard belly?"

"Rock climbing. I find it's good for the gut and relieves stress. The danger makes you focus on the moment."

She lowered her head and began kissing his flushed skin, starting at his flat brown nipples and working her way over the washboard stomach he was suddenly glad he had.

He was no longer able to keep himself from thrusting ever so slightly with his hips as her sweet lips moved inexorably downward to his belt.

He wanted like hell to bury his hands in her curly waves of light brown hair, but he knew he'd break the spell if he did. His hands remained captive beneath his head as he remained captive beneath her marauding lips.

She lifted her head and stared into his eyes, her pupils huge. "Permission to proceed?" she inquired, her hand on his belt buckle.

"As you may have guessed, the word *no* has left my vocabulary. Please," he urged.

She laughed, a throaty laugh full of girlish delight. It made him even harder, and the effect was almost painful.

She undid his belt buckle and pulled the belt from the loops of his trousers. Grinning down at him, she undid the button above the zipper of his fly. "There, more comfy?" she teased.

"Only slightly. If you could, ah, hurry the hell up."

"I've noticed you have this problem with being impatient, Mr. Hawksley. Perhaps we should—"

"Now!" he insisted.

Her answering laugh as she began easing down the zipper of his trousers was wicked with promise.

"You've been holding out on me, Noel. You've been pretending to be a grinch, and all the while you've had a present for me." Her hand closed over the smooth, satiny length of him. "A very, very impressive present."

"Glad you like it," he choked out as she began moving her hand up and down, squeezing and relaxing her grip.

"I like it so much I could kiss you!" she declared. "Right here." She punctuated her statement with a kiss to the head of his shaft, sending a delicious shock of pleasure through him.

And then a noise at the front door woke him.

Noel was disoriented at first. The dream had seemed so real.

So hot. He was still reeling from the effect. It certainly put the lie to any idea that everything between them was strictly business. He was very attracted to her, he admitted with some reluctance. And not just physically attracted. No, Hollie Winslow was reaching him on a level no one ever had.

And then he laughed, rueful that it was probably just business with Hollie. Her niceness was part of her professional image. He was more likely to buy a house from her if he liked her.

He needed to get a grip on reality.

Ah, but he wished she'd be as nice to him as she had been in his dream, he thought as the door swung open.

AS SHE INSERTED the key into the lock of her front door, Hollie shifted the bag on her hip, careful not to break the eggs. Her Christmas watch had told her she'd only been gone a half hour. The snowy day had kept most people at home with last-minute baking and wrapping and decorating. She'd checked out her eggs and a bottle of wine she'd gotten on impulse without having to wait in line.

When she entered the greatroom, Noel was sitting up on the sofa, stretching.

She grimaced, then hurried to the kitchen to set her small bag of groceries on the counter.

A large plastic sack of Tupperware sat there.

"Where did this come from?" she asked Noel, who'd joined her in the kitchen.

"Sarah dropped it off. She said Elena was playing at a friend's house, so she was out running errands while she had the opportunity."

Hollie looked at Noel's face. "She didn't say anything?" she asked.

"Oh, yeah—something about calling her. She needs you to take Elena to see Santa Claus at the mall because she got a big last-minute order."

"That's all she said?" Hollie asked, her head inside the refrigerator as she stowed the eggs and wine.

"Yeah, she mentioned you wanted to borrow the Tupperware and said to call her about Elena, that's all."

Noel looked so sexy and sweet with sleep that Hollie couldn't resist going over to him and kissing him on the tip of his nose.

"What?" Noel said, pleased yet taken aback.

Hollie shrugged. "It's Christmas. You looked so..." Hollie's voice trailed off. What had come over her? Kissing him on the nose? And her explanation would be worse. What was she going to say? That she'd done it because he looked sexy... and sweet?

"Do you always act on your impulses?" Noel asked with a teasing glint in his eyes.

"Do you never have them?" Hollie pouted, her teeth pulling at her full bottom lip, drawing Noel's attention.

He thought about the dream Sarah had interrupted with her Tupperware delivery. He'd been worried she would notice his arousal.

"I guess this wouldn't be a good time to ask you a favor, huh?" Hollie ventured.

"I'm not taking Elena to see Santa Claus, if that's what you have in mind."

"No, I haven't forgotten you're a grinch. What I need is for you to give me some help with the lights on my Christmas tree. There's a short somewhere and they keep going out. I thought perhaps you might be able to figure out what's wrong. I don't know which strand is shorting, and I hate to go out and buy all new lights."

"Sure, I could check them out," he agreed. "It seems we're not going to be busy seeing any houses this afternoon. This looks to be a half-foot-deep snowfall. I suppose you want me to shovel your driveway while I'm at it, too."

"You'd do that?" she asked on a hopeful note. It wasn't as though she was suggesting he help build a snowman, not yet anyway.

"Why not? I might as well. That way I'll know whether this house requires a snow shovel. When it stops snowing I'll do the drive. Right now, let's have a look at the lights on your tree." He headed for the tree in the corner of the room.

"Wait a minute. What did you mean by you'll know whether this house requires a snow shovel?"

"Didn't I mention it? I've found the house I want to buy. *This one.*"

The news was as much a surprise to him as to Hollie. He hadn't known he wanted her house until he'd said it.

But once he'd said it, he knew it was true.

Hollie's house fit the fantasy of a home he'd never had. It was warm and inviting. So inviting he'd fallen asleep on her sofa. Spending time in the place had made him realize the strength of his long suppressed and denied fantasy and desire for a home.

What Hollie had made him realize was what he didn't have.

He'd realized his professional dreams, and maybe, just maybe, it was time he took a look at what his personal needs were.

He had a feeling Hollie could meet a lot of those, had certainly met one of them in his dreams!

She was sexy as all get out, but there was more to this hunger he had. He wanted a soul mate. For the first time in his life he considered that he might have found one...in Hollie.

He wanted to step into her dream. And that meant buying her house.

Meanwhile, back at the North Pole...

"I SURE HOPE Mrs. Claus comes back before we have to leave on Christmas Eve," Rudolph said to Prancer. "Santa's been a grouch ever since he found out she left on her little vacation."

Prancer danced around his stall. "I know one thing— it sure would be a help if he could find the Christmas cookies Mrs. Claus hid before she left."

"I wouldn't count on that..." Rudolph said, his nose turning red.

"Rudolph—you didn't! You didn't find Santa's cookies first and eat them?"

"Who, me?"

Prancer shook his head. "It's going to be a long sleigh ride Christmas Eve."

5

NOEL COULDN'T BELIEVE he was standing in a long line at the mall, waiting to see Santa Claus. But here he was, being pushed and shoved by impatient, restless, jumpy kids desperate to reach Santa and whisper their dream gift list in St. Nick's ear.

Hollie had insisted that he join her and Elena in the Santa line if he wanted to continue their discussion about her selling her house. And since he was as impatient, restless and jumpy to get the opportunity to try one more time to persuade Hollie to sell, he was on his way to Santa...and, hopefully, acquiring Hollie's house.

She'd already said no to him more than once, but for some reason it was important to him to buy her house. Where he lived had never been of consequence to him before. He had moved from one temporary residence to another. First with boarding school and then with his career.

For the first time, he desperately wanted a home. And Hollie's house was it.

Noel studied Hollie and Elena. Both were clearly girlie girls.

Hollie was kneeling to fasten the sparkly tiara Elena had insisted on wearing. It had slipped sideways on the child's head. Fixing the tiara wasn't an easy task because Elena was so excited about seeing Santa she was chattering nonstop, her head moving the whole while.

"How many things can I ask Santa for?" Elena wanted to know. "Will he get mad if I ask for too many?"

"I think three would be a good number," Hollie said dryly. "That's the number that seems standard in any magical situation. Just remember to think about your wishes very carefully while we're waiting. You don't want to waste them on something silly like wishing Midnight would quit barking at airplanes when they fly over."

Elena giggled. "I know, she thinks she can catch them."

Hollie tickled Elena's tummy. Elena's fashion statement for meeting Santa was her tiara, of course. And, of all things, her neon sunglasses in the dead of winter with snow on the ground. The rest of her ensemble consisted of a white T-shirt beneath jeans overalls, black-and-white soccer shoes and all her jeweled necklaces.

Noel couldn't help but smile. Elena's style was utterly charming. She would make a great model for the children's department of the store he was opening.

At least, Noel thought, it was good to see that he wasn't the only male in line waiting with the children to see Santa. All around him fathers were standing patiently, while mothers combed children's hair and straightened their clothing—over and over again as the children continued hopping around. The din from the crowd was so loud he could barely make out Aaron Neville's "Christmas Song" on the mall's sound system.

If anyone had told him he'd willingly be at a mall five days before Christmas, he would have bet a considerable sum otherwise—and lost. He expected to see hives break out on his arm at any time. Last Christmas Marcy had insisted on him shopping with her while she selected the expensive gifts she wanted from him. She hadn't returned the pricey baubles when she'd broken their engagement and had even claimed possession of some of his things.

"I know one thing I'm going to ask Santa for," Elena said, as Noel winced in remembrance. "I'm going to ask him to bring me the Barbie in the pink dress."

Hollie shot Noel a look that told him he was in trouble. But hell, he already knew that. He was standing in a crowded mall with a woman who was something between a ballerina and a kick boxer and a child who would grow up under her influence. "Under the influence" gained a whole new meaning when he thought of Hollie. Under her influence he'd had a dream so sexy he'd woken up embarrassed.

"I'm sure Santa will bring you your Barbie," Noel assured Elena, to Hollie's raised eyebrow. "What else are you going to wish for?"

"I know, I want some rings like Hollie's."

Hollie twisted the gold-and-gemstone stack rings on her ring finger of her right hand. Seeing Noel's interest, she explained, "Elena's coveted these since I bought them this past summer. I told her they don't make them in her small size, so every time she comes over she asks me if they're old yet."

"Old?" Noel looked puzzled

"It's a scam of hers. When she spends the night she goes through my jewelry piece by piece and asks if each one is old. She gets to take anything that's old home with her. You may have noticed she's into jewelry in a big way."

"Yeah. Some husband is going to be perpetually broke when she gets married—"

"What are you going to wish for?" Elena interrupted, looking at Noel.

"That Hollie will sell me her house."

Elena appeared stricken. "No! You can't move away, Auntie Hollie." The child grabbed Hollie's hand and clung to her, a tear trailing from her wide pale eyes.

"Don't worry, I'm *not* moving," she assured the child.

"But—"

"We're going to find Noel a house he really, really likes. He was only teasing about wanting my house."

Noel didn't want to push the matter in front of the upset child. After all, Hollie could move closer to Sarah and Elena. The child would love that. There was even room for Hollie to move in with Sarah and Elena until she found something.

He didn't have anywhere to go.

Unless you counted the impersonal hotel room he was staying in.

"And what are you going to wish for?" Noel asked Hollie.

"That a grinch doesn't spoil my Christmas," she answered, frowning at him.

"What's a grinch, Auntie Hollie?"

"Someone who doesn't like Christmas."

"Oh, you made that up. Everybody loves Christmas." The child didn't even wait for confirmation of her belief. She tugged on Hollie's hand to move them up in line as a flash went off when the child in front of them had his picture taken on Santa's lap.

Noel studied the Santa as the little boy climbed down off his lap and Elena moved to take his place, and thought Santa looked a little seedy, shabby. The whole thing commercial. But Hollie didn't see it that way. She saw the magic. She made the magic.

For herself.

For Elena.

For *him*.

For the first time in his life he wondered what it would be like to have a child. Wondered with his heart, not in an abstract way. The way he might have wondered when he'd become engaged last Christmas. He'd turned thirty and it had seemed time to marry. He'd cared about the woman, but now saw he hadn't been in love.

Love was a much scarier proposition.

He hadn't been this disconcerted since the first time he'd arrived at boarding school. The school had been strict, and military. Emotions weren't encouraged; obedience was.

"Ho, ho, ho. And what do you want Santa to bring you, little girl?"

Elena smiled up at Santa. "I want a Barbie with a pink dress."

"And what else?"

"Some rings, a bunch of little bitty ones."

"Anything else?" Santa asked as the photographer snapped their picture.

Elena thought a minute, then was generous with her third wish. "I want you to bring a boyfriend for my mommy."

"Oh—" Santa said, caught off guard.

Then Elena cupped her hand and whispered something in Santa's ear.

"Of course you can have a fourth wish," Santa said magnanimously, obviously happy to be off the subject of granting the mother a boyfriend, not knowing how appropriate the wish was. "What else do you want?"

"I want you to make Auntie Hollie and him," she said loudly, pointing to Noel, "kiss each other so Auntie Hollie won't have to move away."

It wasn't an easier wish. Santa looked to Noel for help.

The crowd close around looked on in anticipation. The mothers looked hopeful. The fathers looked amused. The children giggled.

When Noel and Hollie remained frozen in place, a father in the crowd yelled out, "Kiss her, for Pete's sake. I've got a hockey game to get my kid to."

Hollie wouldn't look at him. She was sure she was as red as Santa's suit. Most of all because she wanted Noel to kiss her.

Since he'd clearly worried Elena, Noel found himself doing something out of character. Overt displays of public affection weren't his style. He stepped closer to Hollie.

She took a backward step, nervous and looking about to faint.

He handled that by taking her into his arms and dipping her back in a sweeping embrace. As he gazed into her startled eyes, he lowered his mouth and kissed her for the audience and Elena. His mouth moved tenderly over hers, then probed sexily, making her blush and break the kiss, flustered.

Upon hearing the applause, he came to his senses and quickly released Hollie, who appeared completely stunned.

"Thank you, Santa," Elena said, scampering off his lap and grinning widely.

"Are you satisfied now, you little minx?" Hollie asked, taking the child's hand.

"Uh-huh. Noel was just tricking me about buying your house, huh?"

Hollie nodded.

Well, Elena might be satisfied, but Noel decidedly was not. He still wanted the house . . . and more of kissing Hollie. Was it possible he was falling in love?

Or was he just tired of being alone?

He couldn't trust his feelings at this time of year. That was why he always ran away during the holidays.

"Where are we going now?" Elena asked as they left the mall.

"Noel and I are going to look at houses for him, right after I drop you off at home."

"Can't I come with you?"

"No. Your mother says you have to clean your room if you want Santa to bring you any presents. Santa likes good little girls with clean rooms."

"Aw right," Elena agreed reluctantly.

As they drove Elena home, Noel realized he hadn't seen Hollie's bedroom yet.

"MAYBE YOU'LL LIKE this one better," Hollie said as she parked her car and handed Noel the spec sheet to look at while they walked to the front door. So far they'd seen three houses, which he'd vetoed for what seemed to her one frivolous reason after another.

Clearly he was determined to have her house and was only humoring her by looking at others. She'd told him she'd think about selling her house. She'd lied.

Her mind was made up. She loved her house and her house loved her. They were a good match.

And she and Noel weren't, no matter how well he kissed.

She wanted to tell Noel that she couldn't help him any longer, wanted to bail out. What had started out to be a snap had grown complicated.

And now she was stuck. She had to deal with Noel. Her getting a new car was at risk. It didn't look great for a successful real estate agent to be driving around in a wreck. His commission would give her the down payment for a new car.

Her career was at risk. She had to be professional and maintain her reputation as a responsible agent. So there would be no quitting until she found Noel a house.

Her vacation was at risk. The longer it took, the less of the holidays she would be able to enjoy. And at this rate they'd still be looking for a new house for Noel in the New Year.

Her house was at risk.

All of the above could be solved by her selling him her house. But she couldn't and she wouldn't. It was hers. The only roots she had in the world. She felt safe there and happy.

Her heart was at risk.

There, she'd thought it. Of everything, that was the most worrisome. In Noel she recognized a kindred spirit. They didn't look at the world in the same way, but they had experienced loneliness in the same way. She'd determined to make her world a happy place.

He threatened that.

She didn't want to be disappointed, and as long as she was in control she knew how to prevent it.

It was only when she allowed herself to hope that someone might love her that she was vulnerable to misery.

Perhaps that was why she lived with one foot in the real world and one in the world of fantasy. The real world had a way of disappointing her.

"This looks like a place you might like," Noel said when they went inside the story-and-a-half house decorated to within an inch of its life in cluttered country.

"We're hunting for a house for you. I have one I like."

"You aren't even trying to find another house," Noel complained.

"I told you—I don't want to move. Why won't you believe me and accept it? My house isn't that big. There isn't room for a big office or a pool table. This house, on the other hand, fits both those requirements. At least give it a chance."

He walked through it with her, letting her try to sell him on its finer points, such as the study off the master bedroom, the fireplace in the hearth kitchen and the in-ground pool. While he agreed that all those things were pluses, he just didn't love the house.

Not the way he loved hers.

And so they closed the door and left once more, without his making an offer.

And closed the door on her having a long weekend. She was going to have to take Noel out the next day to look at houses again.

So much for her Friday. She'd have to battle the huge crowds on the weekend to get the rest of her holiday preparations done.

She had to find Noel a house.

Someone else's house.

"SO ELENA TELLS ME Noel kissed you at the mall," Sarah said later that evening as the two of them sat in front of the television they weren't watching. Elena was curled up asleep on the floor with Midnight. The child had drifted off watching *Pocahontas* and hadn't awoken when they'd slipped out the tape to turn on the news.

"Did she tell you it was her idea?" Hollie blew on the nails of her left hand after giving them their first coat of polish.

"She left that out. What did she do now?" Sarah was clearly delighted with her daughter's precocious ways.

"She pimped Santa at the mall into making us kiss as one of her wishes. For some reason she thought it would make me not sell my house to Noel."

"When did you decide to sell your house to Noel— did I miss a meeting?" Sarah asked, reaching for a bottle of top coat for her nails.

"I didn't. I'm not. But Noel isn't listening to me. He's got it into his head that he wants to buy it. He's positively fixated on the idea. I'm trying desperately to talk him out of it, to find the perfect house for him."

"But you aren't having any luck..."

"None."

"Hmm. So how does he kiss? You've completely avoided that—don't think I haven't noticed."

"Like he's done it before."

"Smooth, huh?"

"And sweet."

"Sweet—now, that's something new. Sweet, huh?"

"Don't go making anything out of it. He was on the spot. It's not like it was his idea. Or mine," she added, seeing the speculative look in Sarah's eyes.

"Then maybe Elena's smarter than you. He's pretty hunky, Hollie." Sarah put the applicator back in the bottle and studied her manicure.

"Elena's smarter than you and I put together, Sarah. But I'm still not taking dating advice from a four-year-old. Besides, Santa's bringing me a beau for Christmas. All I have to do is get rid of Noel first."

"So sell him your house."

That was the practical answer, Hollie knew.

But she couldn't sell Noel her house. She just couldn't.

There had to be a house out there with his name on it. She just hadn't found it yet. Maybe in the morning when she was fresh . . .

"Did Elena tell you she asked Santa to bring you a boyfriend?" Hollie inquired, changing the subject, as they waited for their nails to dry so they could carry Elena in to bed.

"So that's where he came from—"

"What? You've met someone. You've been holding out on me." Hollie settled back into the sofa, tucking her feet up beneath her.

"He's a fireman and really sweet. He came out this morning to rescue the kitten next door that got stuck up in a tree. He was really good with the kitten and the neighborhood kids. But I think he might be a bit young for me."

"How old is he?"

"I don't know for sure. I think late twenties, maybe."

"Old enough to vote," Hollie said, throwing a pillow at Sarah.

"You're bad."

"Moi?" The women collapsed in girlish giggles that woke up Elena.

"Is Santa here yet?" the child asked, rubbing her sleepy eyes.

"Not yet, sugarpie. You've still got a few days yet to wait for Santa to visit. Christmas isn't until Wednesday. Go back to sleep."

As Hollie lifted the child into her arms, Elena's eyes drifted closed again. Hollie walked with Sarah back to Elena's bedroom, where the two women tucked her in with kisses of good-night and sweet dreams.

"So, what's the fireman's name?" Hollie asked as they left the sleeping child and went back to watching the news, mainly interested in whether there would be more snow for Christmas.

"Rick Winzen."

"So are you going to see him?" Hollie persisted.

"He hasn't asked me out, if that's what you mean."

Hollie laughed. "Since when has that stopped you? So you ask him out."

"I think I might scare him off if I did."

Hollie looked more closely at her friend. Sarah was thirty-five, but appeared ten years younger. Sarah usually went after what she wanted, and usually got it. This hesitancy was new for her friend. There was almost a shyness in Sarah's demeanor.

"He's special, isn't he? You like this Rick Winzen a lot, don't you?"

"Maybe."

"I know, why don't you go see Ms. Claudia and ask her about Rick?"

"Really, Hollie. I've got a schedule that would panic Santa's elves from now to Christmas. Tomorrow I have to spend the whole day making a sit-down dinner for twenty-four to be delivered by seven o'clock. I don't have time for a visit to your favorite psychic. Besides, I'm sure Rick isn't interested in me. He's just a nice guy being polite."

Sarah's disclaimer held a wistful note.

"I think—" Hollie's thought was interrupted by the ringing of the telephone.

"Who could that be?" Sarah said, glancing at the time on the VCR. "It's after ten o'clock."

Since Hollie was nearest the phone, she picked it up. "Just a minute, she's here," she told the caller, and tossed the portable phone to Sarah.

Sarah caught the phone, her eyes questioning.

Hollie silently mouthed the words "It's him."

"Hello..." Sarah said shyly. "Hello, Rick," she added after the caller identified himself.

"Look, I may be being presumptuous here, Sarah, but I didn't see a wedding ring, so I thought maybe there wasn't a Mr. Smith and I was wondering if maybe you'd like to go out tomorrow."

"Tomorrow night? You want to go out tomorrow night?" Sarah grinned from ear to ear at Hollie, who encouraged her by nodding.

"No, not tomorrow night. I have an obligation for tomorrow night I can't get out of. I thought maybe you and Elena would like to have lunch and then go see the *Nutcracker* ballet. My sister can get us tickets."

"Could you hold on a second, Rick." Sarah clutched the phone to her chest so he couldn't hear her. "Hollie, he wants to take Elena and me to see the *Nutcracker* tomorrow!"

"So say yes."

"But I can't. I've got all that food to make for the dinner I'm catering tomorrow night."

"You two go. I'll make the food."

"But what about Noel?"

"I can handle Noel—don't you worry. You need a treat. So go. I'll handle making the food. And then you'll owe me big-time."

Sarah looked uncertain about Hollie's generous offer.

Hollie insisted.

"Rick, we'd love to go," Sarah finally said into the phone she'd returned to her ear. "What time?"

"Let's get an early start. I'll pick you up at eleven."

Sarah pushed the button to disconnect, tossed the phone to Hollie and let out a shriek. "He likes me!"

"Of course he likes you. And now I'm going home. I need a good night's sleep if I'm going to play Martha Stewart tomorrow."

"Oh, Hollie, are you sure about this?"

"Let me go before I come to my senses," Hollie teased, pulling on her coat.

"But what about Noel?"

"I'll tell him I had a little emergency and he'll adjust."

"But it's not going to endear you to him."

"Sarah, I don't think you can endear yourself to a grinch."

"Maybe he's not really such a grinch."

"Goodbye, Sarah."

"Bye."

Hollie hurried to her car, not wanting to remember that Noel certainly hadn't kissed like a grinch.

NOEL SAT ON THE BED in his room with the newspaper spread out around him. He was studying his competition. The papers were full of holiday ads and he could glean which store carried what merchandise and where each store focused their advertising for their market share.

He'd tried to distract himself at first with the television, but it was full of holiday specials, everything from old Bing Crosby repeats to a country gala. And the commercials were worse.

The newspaper ads were equally festive, but he could at least detach himself enough to study them with an eye to business.

But even the ads didn't hold his attention for very long. Soon his thoughts were back to the problem at hand.

He couldn't understand why Hollie was being so stubborn about selling him her house. She had even rejected his offer to pay her moving costs... rejected his second offer that was more than the fair market price.

How could anyone be such a bad businesswoman?

She needed the money to buy a new car; even he could see that.

He was beginning to think her refusal was personal. He had the fanciful thought that she didn't want him living in her house. And he didn't ever have fanciful thoughts.

But what else could he think when she continued to refuse to sell her house to him?

Maybe what he needed to do was mount a campaign to make her like him better. Perhaps then she'd feel okay about selling him her house. He never would have thought he'd have to pass muster to buy something.

It was worth a try. Otherwise, he had the sinking feeling that he was going to be stuck in the States for the entire holiday season.

What, he wondered, would make Hollie approve of him buying her house?

He began drawing up a list of possibilities.

Having a plan made him confident that in a day or so he'd be relaxing in the islands, with a house to return to in the new year.

Meanwhile, back at the North Pole...

SANTA SAT AT HIS computer playing a game, one he'd invented with reindeer navigating an obstacle course. He'd been playing half the night.

His thumb was getting numb.

The mindless activity was his way of escaping the stress of having a missing wife.

He was going to have to get his act together and take it on the road soon or a lot of little boys and girls were going to vote the Easter bunny top good guy.

6

December 21

HOLLIE HAD HOPED she'd have a day without Noel.

Just her luck, when she'd called to cancel looking at houses with him, he'd suggested he come over to Sarah's to help her so she would be done in half the time and there would still be a few hours for them to find a house for *her*. Like a tenacious dog with a bone, he wasn't giving up. He really believed he could convince her to sell him her place.

She saw his car pull up in Sarah's driveway as she began making an assembly line on the counter to put together the rolled breakfast steaks called rouladen. He was probably going to slow her down, since she imagined his primary contact with food had been in restaurants. She noted his car had been restored to its classic elegant line—all traces of the fender bender vanished. Her insurance had covered it.

He was as elegant as his car. Even casually dressed in slacks and a blue sweater beneath his bomber jacket, he appeared sleek and powerfully sexy.

Midnight set up a racket when she heard the door-bell, but went back to her usual spot by the picture window watching the birds at the feeder when Hollie shooed her away.

When Noel entered the house, he began to walk in the direction of the kitchen. "The TV is in there, if you re-call," Hollie said, pointing to the living room.

"But I came to help," Noel insisted.

"I thought you were kidding."

He just stared at her. "I never kid."

"I should know that by now. What must I have been thinking? Okay, hang your jacket in the closet, push up your sleeves and I'll put you to work."

Why hadn't she said no from the start? Hollie chastised herself. She hadn't liked how much she'd liked seeing him. Was used to seeing him every day. It occurred to her that she was going to miss him when he left...if he ever did. She had never had a client quite like him. And she had never gotten so involved with one.

"What do you want me to do?"

Noel's words filtered into her musing and she caught herself before she said, *Kiss me again the way you did at the mall.* What was wrong with her?

"Do the bacon strips in the microwave," she ordered. "I'll get the other ingredients ready while you're doing that."

Hollie took off her stack rings and laid them on the countertop out of the way. She focused on the task at hand, deliberately ignoring how good Noel smelled, and how disturbing and unnerving having him so close by was.

She got out the Italian bread crumbs and the Italian salad dressing and put both into deep bowls. She added a large package of shredded cheese to another bowl and then began shredding a dozen carrots.

When Noel had the bacon crisped, she showed him how to make the rouladens; demonstrating with one breakfast steak, she dipped it first in the Italian salad dressing, then in the Italian bread crumbs. Next she placed a piece of crisp bacon in the middle of the steak and added the shredded cheese and grated carrots by the heaping tablespoon. The finishing touch was rolling the stuffed strips up, jelly-roll fashion, and securing them with three toothpicks per rouladen.

"If you assemble the rouladens, I'll make a big pan of gravy to bake them in. Think you can manage—and aren't you sorry you offered to help?"

"I can manage," he assured her.

They worked in companionable silence, both lost in their own thoughts.

He finally interrupted her with a question.

"So how did you get into real estate?"

"I've always loved houses and I guess I just sort of drifted into it," Hollie answered, stirring the gravy continuously.

"It seems like a pretty tough way to make a living," he observed. "Don't you have to take a lot of grief from customers?"

"You may have noticed an agent learns to let the customer's frustration slide off—most of the time. It's tenacity that gets the sale. You have to be prepared to make sales calls and follow-up calls or face losing potential customers to another agent."

He was quiet for a moment, as he absorbed her answer.

"Why? Are you thinking of taking it up?" Hollie asked, turning up the gas flame beneath the pan of gravy.

"Not a chance. I don't enjoy working with the public."

"Good choice, because you'd kill your clients when they changed their minds for the thirty-eighth time."

"Is that a dig?"

"No, you've made up your mind. I'm working on changing it."

"Why are you so stubborn?"

"Me?" She frowned.

"Yes, you. I'm offering you more money than your house is worth."

"You can't put a monetary value on some things. But I guess when you come from a wealthy background the way you do you wouldn't know that."

UPS drove up at that moment, and the deliveryman ran up the walk and rang the doorbell. Midnight began barking and Hollie dropped the spoon she was stirring the gravy with into the pan of hot liquid. She swore beneath her breath, momentarily flustered.

"I'll get the door," Noel offered, washing off his hands and grabbing a towel as he headed for the front door. "You deal with the dog."

Midnight escaped Hollie's lunge and raced out the door between Noel's legs when Noel opened the door.

"Midnight!" Hollie yelled after the fleeing dog.

The dog had a taste of freedom and was scampering away across the muddy lawn as fast as its little feet would go. The ever changing St. Louis weather had turned warmer, melting the snow that had previously fallen.

"You sign for the package and I'll go get the dog," Noel ordered, taking charge.

"But—"

"I don't know what to do in the kitchen without you," Noel rationalized. "It shouldn't take me long to retrieve Midnight. She's just a little bit of a thing."

As Noel took off after Midnight, Hollie didn't have the heart to tell him that he'd met his match, little bitty or not.

"Ma'am?" The deliveryman was in a hurry. The preholiday schedule had him swinging double shifts.

Hollie signed for the package for Sarah and went back to the kitchen. She had mounds of spuds to peel for the mashed potatoes to go with the rouladens. Trust a man to disappear when the drudgery part of cooking arrived.

"DAMN IT," Noel swore as his loafers hit a slick patch of muddy lawn and he went sprawling.

Midnight barked at him and scampered beyond his reach.

Noel scowled at the little piece of fluff, then down at his ruined slacks. A large grass stain covered one knee and his hand hurt where it had landed on a rock, scraping off some skin.

"Come here, Midnight," he said in a tone that meant business.

No response.

"I said, come here."

Midnight barked again and began walking away.

The stupid mutt thought they were playing a game, Noel soon realized. It would serve the animal right if he just left her outside until she got hungry enough to come home. But it might be a while. Midnight was well fed and used to being outside in the fenced yard. The delicious taste of freedom wasn't something she'd give up so easily.

Noel couldn't abandon the silly dog, because the animal was dumb enough to run out in front of a car. But it didn't keep him from feeling like a fool, he grumbled as he rose to chase the creature. It wasn't seemly. If the dog were a German shepherd or something, okay. But a wee little dog made him look ridiculous.

Still, Elena would be distraught if she returned home and her dog was missing, so he continued chasing Midnight.

"Come here, girl," Noel called, trying ever so discreetly to inch closer and closer to the dog without Midnight noticing what Noel was doing. How hard could it be to catch such a little bitty thing? He was certainly not about to be outsmarted by a piece of fluff.

Midnight sat down and waited, watching Noel's slow approach. She cocked her head and listened to him coax her to come to him.

"That's it, girl. Just sit very still until I reach you and pick you up ever so gently and wring your silly little neck."

But just as soon as Noel got within lunging distance of Midnight, the dog would bounce away as though she were on tiny springs, then bark at him from a safe distance, as if Noel were some mean old dognapper.

Frustrated, Noel tried flat out running after the scampering dog and nearly knocked himself out when he ran smack into a low tree branch; he actually saw a burst of tiny stars momentarily. Feeling a little dizzy, he stayed put where he'd landed on the ground.

Which was what he should have done all along, because Midnight began whining and walked back over to him, jumping into Noel's lap and licking his face.

But a couple of neighborhood kids riding by on their bikes attracted Midnight's attention and the dog leaped from Noel's grasp to take off after the boys, yapping at their feet.

Noel held his head in his hands, wishing he were on a warm sunny island with his head hurting because he was hung over.

He had to get up and go after the dog.

Before he lost sight of it.

Sound of it, anyway.

Pushing himself up off the damp ground, he resumed the chase.

NOEL HAD BEEN GONE a long time, Hollie thought uneasily.

She prayed nothing had happened to Midnight. Elena would be upset and her holiday would be completely ruined.

She emptied the boiling water from the large stockpot full of potatoes and shook them into a bowl for whipping.

By the time she'd finished making the mashed potatoes and checked on the rouladens in the oven, Noel and Midnight still had not returned.

Her worry increased as she worked to make the rest of the dishes for the dinner party Sarah was catering. Helping Sarah from time to time had taught her a lot about catering.

She checked her watch. "Where are you, Noel?" she asked aloud. Sarah and Elena weren't due back for a while, but that still didn't prevent Hollie from worrying.

To distract herself, she went to the stereo system and put on the radio, turning from a talk radio station to a station playing Christmas carols.

Returning to the refrigerator, she got out the endive bunches, red leaf lettuce and romaine to wash for the tub of salad. While her hands were busy with the idle task of rinsing the lettuce, she let herself itemize the holiday tasks she had yet to do. First on the list was finding the Barbie in the pink dress for Elena.

Then she wanted to try making sugared fruit. Oh, yes, she needed to get the makings for a gingerbread house because she'd promised Elena she could spend the night and they would make one together. And as of yet, she hadn't found the special ornament for this year to add to the tree, a custom she'd started when she'd bought the house.

She let out a little gasp, suddenly remembering she'd forgotten to kiss a pomegranate on December 15, which would have meant all her Christmas wishes would come true. Instead she'd kissed a grinch—it was impossible to know what that meant.

Noel could have easily spent the day doing something besides helping her cook and, now, chasing down Midnight. Was he trying to get into her good graces so she'd sell the house to him? He'd claimed he was helping so they could look at some houses later in the day. But she wondered if the real reason he'd offered was that he was lonely.

She'd just finished the lettuce and drained the water, when the doorbell rang. Wiping her hands dry on a dish towel, she went to get the door, hoping it was Noel with Midnight.

Her hopes were answered. Midnight was squirming, but safe and sound in Noel's arms. Noel, however, looked as though he'd been hit by a truck.

"What happened to you?" she cried, taking the dog as Noel came inside. "Are you all right?"

"I need to sit down."

She helped Noel to the sofa, while Midnight made her way to her water dish and lapped loudly.

Noel gingerly lowered himself to the sofa. "Can you turn off the music, please? And turn out the lights."

Hollie hurried to do as he requested. Midnight, tired from her adventure, headed for the bed in Elena's room.

"What happened to you?" Hollie asked again when she returned to Noel's side.

"A low branch knocked me senseless when I was chasing that, that...dog! And then I had to crawl under a car to get her in the end."

"I'm so sorry, Noel. Can I do anything for you?"

"As a matter of fact, you can. I'm prone to tension headaches and I've got a prescription to pick up." He reached in his pants pocket to withdraw his wallet. "Here, take this. There's cash and my insurance card. Those pills should take care of this headache. I'll just wait here until you get back."

"Will you be okay by yourself? You could have a concussion or something," she said with concern.

"No, I'm fine. I've got a goose egg on my forehead and a headache, but I'm not dizzy or nauseous. If you'll just fetch me my prescription from Walgreens on Lindbergh, I'll be fine."

She took his wallet and jotted down her cell phone number on her business card, then placed the card on the table beside him. "You can reach me on my cell phone if you need me," she said, retrieving the portable phone and setting it beside the business card.

"Thanks."

Hollie checked the rouladens in the oven to make sure they were ready, then turned off the oven.

"Okay, I'm leaving now," she told him, heading for the front door.

"It smells good in here," he mumbled as she left.

Since it was the last Saturday before Christmas the roads as well as the stores were packed. The drugstore was no exception. There was a long line and a long wait.

Standing in line, Hollie began looking through Noel's wallet for his insurance card. She sorted through a gas credit card, VISA, ATM card and an American Express card, before finding his insurance card. As she was putting the others back in their slots, his driver's license caught her eye.

No, it couldn't be. He was taller. Or shorter.

People lied on their driver's licenses, didn't they?

But in her heart she knew the driver's license wasn't a lie.

Knew it was true.

That Noel Hawksley was a six-foot-one-inch grinch.

"Next," the pharmacist called out, and she moved to the counter to be waited on.

THE WHOLE TRIP had taken Hollie an hour. When she returned to Sarah's, Noel was sleeping restfully on the sofa where she'd left him. She touched the bump that had risen on his forehead and winced at its size. Poor Noel! He must have taken quite a knock on the head.

After leaving the sack from the pharmacy on the coffee table, she returned to the kitchen to finish the catered meal for twenty-four. Midnight had come trotting out when she'd returned, recognized her and then lain in a corner of the kitchen, hoping for a bite or two of what smelled so good.

"You don't deserve a treat," she admonished the expectant dog.

Midnight barked and got her way, sort of.

Hollie rummaged around in the cabinets and found a dog treat to shut her up so she wouldn't wake Noel.

She wanted to think about things before she faced him again with her new knowledge that he was the beau Santa was bringing her for Christmas. She wasn't sure how she felt about it.

Taking several bunches of carrots from the refrigerator, she began peeling them, readying them for the food processor to make a vegetable dish of sliced carrots and snap peas.

Noel was certainly handsome. And he was tall. Six foot one inch. Smart. Successful. Heroic for rescuing Elena's mutt. He had a lot of admirable qualities.

But underneath he was a grinch.

And that just wouldn't do for her.

She insisted her life be sunny-side up. She didn't let her own unhappy past infringe on her present life. Instead she set about trying to make her life as filled with joy and love and good friends and good times as possible.

It was true, she didn't have a lot of money. But she was happy.

She hadn't allowed herself to have a pity party over life's disappointments. That was the road to Grinchville.

Well, at any rate, at least she knew Santa Claus had a major sense of humor. "Ha, ha," she mumbled.

"What's so funny?"

She jumped, startled that Noel was up and about. He had the sack from the pharmacy in his hand.

"Can I get you something?" she asked. "Are you sure you should be up?"

He leaned against the counter. "What smells so good?"

"The rouladens. Which reminds me, I've got to take them out of the oven." As she reached for the oven mitts to do just that, Noel ripped open the sack from the pharmacy and took out his prescription medicine for his headache.

"Where're the glasses?"

Hollie opened the cabinet and handed him one.

He ran the tap water while he opened the plastic bottle and shook out two pills. He tossed them in his mouth and washed them down with a glass of water, then set the empty glass down and rubbed the back of his neck. "I think I'll pass on looking at any houses today. We can start fresh in the morning, if that's all right with you."

"Do you want me to drive you back to the hotel?"

"No. I'm fine. All I need is a soak in a hot tub and some sleep. I'll call you in the morning."

With a muttered expletive at Midnight, Noel donned his jacket and left.

Unperturbed, Midnight continued lying where she was, a "who, me?" look on her face.

Hollie laughed. "Don't look so innocent. You're a very bad doggie."

All her reprimand got Hollie was a wag of the unrepentant dog's tail.

Hollie shook her head at Midnight and went to turn the music back on. Singing along with the Christmas carols, she finished the catered meal according to the notes Sarah had left for her. Finally she had everything ready for Sarah to deliver and thought that Noel's idea of a long soak in a hot tub had a lot of appeal.

While she waited for Sarah and Elena to return she called the number she remembered having put in her purse for the owner of the gingerbread house.

But there was no answer.

By the time Sarah and Elena returned, she had the kitchen cleaned up and was watching the evening news on television.

It was, Hollie decided, a toss-up over whose eyes held the most excitement over the afternoon outing, Sarah's or Elena's.

Finally she saw the reason she'd waited for Sarah's return.

Rick Winzen stepped into the kitchen. He had puppy-dog friendly brown eyes and muscles.

"Hi, I'm Rick," he offered without any prompting.

"I'm Hollie," she said, shaking his hand, which eclipsed hers.

"You're Auntie Hollie," Elena piped up.

"Only to you, sugarpie. So did you like the *Nut-cracker?*" Hollie asked.

"It was beautiful," Sarah enthused.

"I'm going to be a ballerina," Elena insisted, twirling in an arabesque pose.

"It's nice to meet you, Hollie, but I've got to run," Rick said. "I didn't realize traffic would be this bad. There's a charity event down at the firehouse for underprivileged kids."

"Bye," Elena said, looking up from patting Midnight.

"Aren't you forgetting something?" Sarah coached.

"Oh, yeah, I had a really good time, Rick. Thank you for inviting me."

"You're welcome. I'll pick you up at seven tomorrow night, for our date," Rick reminded Sarah.

"You *are* still having Elena spend the night tomorrow?" Sarah asked Hollie as Rick left. "If not, I can try to get a baby-sitter."

"Right on the last Sunday night before Christmas? No, I promised Elena we'd make a gingerbread house, though it's been so crazy that maybe we'll settle for gingerbread men."

"Why is Midnight all muddy?" Elena asked.

"She got out and she needs a bath," Hollie answered.

"She got out? How did you ever get her back?" Sarah asked.

"We'll have to ask Noel that. But I don't think we'll ask him right away."

Especially not when every time she thought of a long, hot soak, she thought of Noel relaxing in the tub—naked.

"Did you have any trouble with the food?" Sarah peeked into the silver foil containers and tubs Hollie had packed the dinner in.

"Nope. Piece of cake. By the way, I do hope you weren't furnishing the dessert, because you didn't leave me any instructions for it."

"Krausse is doing the cake. It will be beautiful. Her stuff is almost too beautiful to eat. You should have seen the chocolate statue she did for a wedding at the zoo."

"Speaking of delicious," Hollie teased.

"What?" Sarah blushed.

"You know what. Rick the cutiepie fireman what."

"You think he's cute."

"Very."

"Yeah, me, too."

"And you have a second date. Fast worker. He must be smitten."

"What's 'smitten'?" Elena piped up.

"Umm...it means when somebody likes you."

"You mean like Noel likes you?"

"Who told you that?" Hollie asked, probing.

"Nobody. I just know."

"Everybody knows but you," Sarah said.

And Hollie threw the oven mitt at her.

"OH, AH, OHHHHH..." Noel groaned as he lowered himself into a tub of hot bathwater to soak his achy bones. He felt as though he'd gone a full quarter with the Rams football team instead of a diminutive little dog.

At least his headache was fading.

He couldn't believe making Hollie like him was this painful. He hoped he'd scored enough points with her to make it worth his pain. And now he was hungry. Probably from smelling all the good food Hollie had been cooking. Perhaps if he leaned on her sympathy, he'd get an invitation out of this for a home-cooked meal.

Tomorrow night, after they looked at some houses, was going to be his time with Hollie. She owed him that much.

He'd earned it.

He settled back into the tub and smiled.

Yes, tomorrow night he and Hollie were going to follow up on that kiss they'd shared.

Meanwhile, back at the North Pole...

SANTA GROANED AS he lowered himself into the outdoor hot tub surrounded by snowdrifts.

He was tired and cranky. Nothing was the same without Claudia.

Especially not the hot tub.

He stretched out in the water and let his mind wander back to a particular starry night they'd shared that had started on the snowmobiles and ended in the hot tub.

The steam rose off the water into the frigid night air as he wondered where that infuriating woman of his was.

He'd gotten her point. It was past time for her to return home.

He missed her, damn it.

7

December 22

"THIS HOUSE IS perfect for you," Noel insisted. "Look at the cathedral ceiling in the greatroom. You could put up as tall a Christmas tree as you want."

"I have a house." She threw out her arms to indicate the expanse of the room. "*You* could easily put a regulation-size pool table here."

He ignored her. "Look at this kitchen," he insisted. "It's a custom-designed gourmet kitchen. You're a fabulous cook, if the aromas I smelled yesterday are any indication of your culinary skills. It's got a double oven, a convection oven and an oversize microwave. You can bake Christmas cookies to your heart's content. The range is a six-burner restaurant-style. It's lost on me because all I do is plug in the coffeemaker."

"I have a house." She wasn't budging.

"Not if I buy it." He crossed his arms in front of his chest, indicating he wasn't budging one little inch, either.

"Come on, Noel. My feet hurt," she moaned, stepping out of her ivory silk heels with the classic bows.

She'd paid too much for them, but since Elena kept asking her if they were old, she knew they were worth it. They made her feel confident. She had worn them for that very reason. She was determined to find Noel a house today—end of story.

"My head hurts," Noel countered. "And it's all your fault."

The rat was playing on her guilt over his misadventure with Midnight. Well, she wasn't going to let him get away with it.

"Okay, let's go. I've been saving the best for last. You're going to love this house," she insisted, slipping back into her shoes.

"Don't count your commission just yet," he grumbled, following her out the front door.

"If you want to get to the islands before Christmas you'd better get in a buying mood fast, because this is about it when it comes to available houses that fit your wish list," she warned. "In case you've lost track of time because you're having so much fun—there's only one day left until Christmas Eve."

"Only two shopping days left until Christmas. I know, I know." He grimaced. "You can't turn around without being bombarded by the date."

"Speaking of shopping, we have to make a stop at Julian's on the way to this last house."

"Your hairdresser?" he guessed.

"Shoe boutique. They finally got in the pair of shoes in my size that I want for Christmas."

"What, do they have little jingle bells on them?" he asked, grumpy and rubbing his sore head.

"No. They're white satin with ankle straps and tiny rosebuds."

"I'll wait in the car." He slid down in the seat and closed his eyes.

She was glad he waited in the car. That way no one was there to raise an eyebrow at her when she impulsively added a pair of daring red sling-backs to her bill. "Merry Christmas, Hollie," she said beneath her breath. Now she really had to get that commission by selling Noel a house. There was no incentive like a little indulgent shopping.

Stowing the shoe boxes in the trunk, she saw the little baskets she'd bought in which to pack the holiday bread she'd baked for the neighbors. She was way behind schedule on her Christmas preparations. Making a mental note to remember the baskets, she slammed the trunk with conviction. He was going to buy this house or else.

"Something wrong with the shoes?" Noel slid her a questioning look as she got back in the car.

"No, why?"

"Well, the way you slammed the trunk, I figured maybe there was a problem."

There was a problem and he was it. But she refrained from pointing that out to him, her discipline as a real estate agent coming to her aid—holding your tongue when you felt like screaming was one of the top ten requirements of a successful agent.

"By the way, you can cross one thing off your list," he said when she didn't answer. "I located a Barbie doll with a pink dress."

That got her attention. "How? I've looked everywhere. It's *the* toy this season and there isn't one to be found," she insisted.

"I'm in retail, remember. I know where to shop, and how."

"Yep, you just lift what you want and try not to get caught sneaking out of the store," she couldn't resist teasing.

"Don't remind me. I called in a favor, okay? So don't worry about the doll. It's on its way by courier and will be here in time for you to give it to Elena for Christmas."

"You still have to buy this house." Pulling over to the exit ramp, Hollie navigated a few lefts and had them going up the secluded drive to the house on Mistletoe Lane. She hoped he didn't notice the name of the street. Noel Hawksley probably wouldn't enjoy living in a place that constantly reminded him of the holidays.

"It's secluded so no one will disturb you while you're working or destressing at the pool table," Hollie said, beginning her pitch as they got out of the car and made their way to the house.

"And I'm trapped if the snowplow doesn't show up," Noel countered.

"The grade of the drive isn't that steep that you'll need a snowplow to get out." Hollie took her key for the lock out of her briefcase as they reached the solid oak doors with etched-glass inserts. "It's close to all the major arteries, so driving to the store you're opening won't take long. Neither will getting to a Rams game or the airport."

"Location, location, location—the real estate agent's creed, right?"

"Right. That means great resale value. And this house has just come on the market. You're going to have to snap it up before anyone else sees it. It's going to go fast. Right now we're in a seller's market. That's why you lost the first house you put in an offer on."

"We'll see."

His noncommittal attitude did not bode well, but Hollie chose to ignore it. She was going to sell him the house because it was right for him. And because if he got out of town before Christmas, it meant there was a more palatable six-foot-one-inch beau on his way from Santa.

She wished she'd never seen Noel's driver's license, because it only intensified her already too strong attraction to him. She didn't want to get involved with a great pair of broad shoulders, smoldering blue eyes, a rock-hard muscular body that would ruin her holiday. Even if he made her heart pound and made her daydream way too frequently about what it would be like to have those large, long-fingered hands of his roaming over her body, exploring and caressing. No matter how great the temptation. She wasn't about to allow his negativity to overwhelm her efforts to make the best of her life by being upbeat. Noel Hawksley just couldn't be Santa's idea of the perfect beau for her—even if he did have a sweet, heroic side to him. That side was only a *side,* she reminded herself.

They stood for a moment in the house. It had oversize natural clay tiles and was big enough to hold the statue of a wild horse pawing the air, which sat next to the stairs that led to the second floor.

"Isn't this spectacular?" Hollie said as they entered far enough into the foyer to see the two-story living room that offered a floor-to-ceiling view of the woods it overlooked.

"I like the horse," was all Noel would admit.

"Maybe we can get the owners to throw it in," Hollie said, not to be dissuaded as she stepped down the two steps to the sunken living room.

He followed her, dragging his feet. "It's awfully bright in here."

"Yes. Isn't it wonderful?"

She'd purposely taken his complaint as praise for the room. "And look over here. There's a screened-in sunroom. It's a perfect place for a picnic on a rainy day."

He grumbled something unintelligible.

"The kitchen's through here," Hollie called out to Noel, who stood staring out the screened sunroom into the dark woods at the edge of the sloping lawn.

"Noel?"

"Coming." He broke away from whatever called him in the darkness to join Hollie in the kitchen.

"While it isn't terribly large, it is efficient. And it has a built-in microwave. The counters are ceramic tile and all the appliances are top of the line and only two years old.''

He nodded noncommittally.

She couldn't get a read on him. He was purposely keeping her in the dark about his response to the house.

"The bedrooms are upstairs, I assume?"

"The master bedroom is on the first floor and the guest bedroom and additional bedrooms are on the second floor. There's also a loft that overlooks the living room. It's the perfect place for your pool table and big-screen television. Shall we have a look?"

Without waiting for his answer, she went through the foyer and began climbing the stairs. She heard his step on the stairs behind her.

When they reached the second floor they were standing directly in the large loft. It had the same view as the living room and from it they could see the pool.

"It's not bad," he conceded.

They did a quick tour of the second-floor bedrooms and baths, then headed back downstairs to check out the master bedroom.

It was oversize, with a walk-in closet as big as a normal bedroom.

"Is there an echo in here when I talk?" Noel asked, commenting on the sheer expanse of space.

Wickedly, Hollie wondered if Noel fancied hearing the sound of his name echoing in the bedroom.

"What are you thinking?" he asked, noticing the smile on her face.

Caught out, she made up a hasty lie. "I wasn't going to mention it, but it'll cost you a mint to mirror the ceiling." And then realized her lie was as bad as her thought.

"Why, Ms. Winslow!"

Wanting to distract him, she headed for the impressive bath with a double shower that looked too inviting. She focused on the oversize tub. "This will accommodate your six-foot-one-inch frame," she informed him without thinking.

"What—did you measure me or something?"

"Oh...oh. Ah, I just happened to see your driver's license when I was looking for your insurance card."

He let her hang for a few seconds and then made her embarrassment worse. "So now you know all the intimate details about me," he teased.

Was it her, or had he moved closer?

They both looked at each other in one of those moments that could lead to loss of control; to acting on the simmering attraction between them.

He lifted his hand to her face and she stood stock-still, breathless.

"You've an eyelash on your cheek," he explained, brushing it away.

He stepped back then, diffusing the tension of the moment. But the attraction was still there...lurking.

"Um...would you like to see the garage?" she asked, her voice cracking, giving her away.

"Yeah, why don't we do that?"

She forced herself not to run from the master bedroom as she turned away from him. She had been that close to doing something really foolish. If only Elena hadn't forced that kiss between them. It kept whispering suggestive ideas in her mind.

The garage was angled to the left side of the house and a basketball hoop hung above the garage door.

He picked up the basketball lying on the driveway and dribbled it, then shot a hoop. Then he turned to her with a grin and asked provocatively, "Want to go one-on-one? You aren't afraid of me, are you?" he challenged.

"I don't play basketball in heels, thank you."

"So take them off." He dribbled around her and threw another hoop, sinking the ball.

"I'll ruin my hose."

"So take them off."

"I don't think so. I've played games with you before, Noel. You're ruthless about winning."

He stopped dribbling and balanced the ball on his hip with his hand. "Why else would you play?"

She shrugged. "I admit I'm as competitive as the next person. I like to win. But I also really like the sheer joy of playing. Having a good time. Everything doesn't have to be about competition. Sometimes the fun is in the playing."

"So you don't care if you sell me this house, then. Is that right?" he asked, baiting her.

"No. I'm not playing a game here, Noel. This is what I do. It's my career. You wanted me to find you a house. I have. It's time you made a decision about it."

Noel dropped the ball and let it roll to the side of the driveway. "Boy, you're some closer. That's it? Take it or leave it?"

"I told you I don't have anything else to show you."

His eyes said that was debatable, but he knew better than to push any more of her buttons.

"Okay, I'll tell you what. I haven't really seen your house, just part of it. Why don't you take me home with you and I'll decide between the two houses."

It was certainly a step forward, Hollie had to admit, even if she wasn't crazy about showing him the rest of her house. But perhaps if she humored him and played along with his request, she'd be able to convince him to make an offer on this house and then she'd be done with Noel.

"I'll show you my place," she agreed. "But I'm not selling it." It wouldn't be fair to give him the wrong impression. Even though she knew he didn't pay the least heed to her refusal to sell. Evidently, he thought he could wear her down. Or maybe even charm her into doing what he wanted.

"I'd just like to look . . ."

And why did everything he say sound as though he were talking about sex?

Or was that just her?

"Speaking of looking... Do you want to see the basement or the grounds here before we leave? That way you won't have any unanswered questions later."

He let her finish showing him around, without further comment. He seemed to be planning something. She hoped it had to do with signing an offer on the house.

When they got in the car and headed down the long drive, he asked, "Do you like it?"

"It doesn't matter if I like it."

"It does to me."

"Then I like it. I'd buy it myself if I could afford it, okay?"

"What was your favorite thing about the house?"

"The French doors leading from the master bedroom to the pool."

"Umm...a romantic touch, I agree."

Was he thinking the same thing she was? That it would be convenient for a late-night swim that would lead to skinny-dipping that would lead to—

"It's been a long day and neither of us had lunch. Why don't I take you out to dinner and then we'll go back to your place?"

It was her. She'd been thinking of seduction and he'd been thinking of food. "We can't go out to dinner tonight, because I've got plans."

He was very quiet, then he sighed. "Oh, you've got a date, then."

She nodded and pulled onto the service road to the highway. "Yes, with a four-year-old. Elena's spending the night. I'm going to have to swing by now and pick her up because Sarah's got a date."

"So I'll take you both out to dinner. I'll even let Elena choose."

"No, you won't, unless you'd actually enjoy going to Honey Bear's Pizza Cave to watch the dancing costumed bears."

"I'm thinking letting her choose is not cool."

Both had figured without the princess of whine. Elena had pestered them until they wound up at Honey Bear's. It worked out okay because they were hungry and the food was fast and tasty, if a tad juvenile. The pizzas were shaped in bear claws and beehives. They even had a dessert pizza, which made Noel look a little green when it passed by on its way to another table.

When they left, Elena shoved all her paper goodies into her teddy bear backpack. In the car on the ride back to Hollie's she was a chatterbox, happy at having gotten her way.

Hollie was going to be just as happy if she, too, got her way tonight and Noel made an offer on the house on Mistletoe Lane.

"Are we going to make a gingerbread house?" Elena asked when they were back at Hollie's.

Hollie ruffled Elena's hair. "There's been a little change in plans, sugarpie. We're going to make snowflakes, instead, because Noel and I spent too much time looking at houses."

"Snowflakes?"

"Yes, they're these pretty powdered-sugar, snow-flake-shaped cookies. I've got a snowman tin we can put some in and you can give them to your mom for Christmas, okay?"

"Yeah." Elena scampered off to put her teddy bear on the bed.

Noel took Hollie's hand, tugging playfully. "Hi, remember me. You were going to show me the house."

"Right. But we have to be careful. I don't want Elena getting upset about me moving again. Why don't I let Elena show you the house?" she suggested just as the little girl came down the hall.

"Elena, would you give Noel a tour of the house while I get everything ready to make the snowflakes?"

"Sure," Elena agreed, taking Noel's hand and leading him back to the room she'd just come from.

"This is my room when I stay over with Auntie Hollie." Elena went to the bed, sat on it and bounced up and down. "I helped her paint it my favorite color. She said it's called straw color."

Noel studied the pale yellow room. A full-length mirror leaned against one wall, and hats and purses and shoes with heels were scattered all around it.

"Those are Hollie's old things she lets me dress up in when I come over. Do you like my new dress?" Elena tucked her fingers beneath the red-and-white gingham pinafore she wore with white long underwear. On her feet were hiking boots that lace-edged socks peeked over.

"I like your dress. Are those your favorite books?" he asked, nodding to a stack beside the bed.

"Uh-huh, these two are my very favorites," she explained, handing him *Gilly, the Seasick Fish* by Susann Batson and *Snickerdoodle Is Not a Cookie* by Bonnie Jeanne Perry. "Will you read them to me?"

"Why don't you show me the rest of the house and I'll read them to you later, after you've made the snowflake cookies with Hollie?" He had to get this kid to sleep.

"Okay. Come on, I'll show you Hollie's bedroom."

Good, Noel thought, relishing finally seeing Hollie's bedroom. Elena was a glitch in his plan for the evening, but the child had to go to sleep sometime. And then he'd have Auntie Hollie's undivided attention.

Elena tucked her hand in Noel's and tugged him along the hall until they reached Hollie's bedroom. "It's really pretty," she declared.

The child was right. It was decorated in soft ice-cream shades. He chuckled when he saw the miniature Christmas tree with lights and tinsel on the night table by her bed.

Elena went over to it and plugged it in, her eyes lighting up. "Auntie Hollie has her very own bedroom tree. I'm going to have one, too, when I get big."

"I bet you are," Noel agreed.

There was a scurry on the roof and Elena's eyes got very big. "Do you think it's Santa's reindeer already?"

Noel laughed. "No, I don't think they make a practice run. Christmas Eve is pretty much it, as far as I know."

"Oh." She went to bounce on Hollie's bed, seeming to find it impossible to pass a bed without bouncing on it.

"Auntie Hollie's bed is the softest bed ever."

It looked it, he thought. It was covered with a pale pink comforter, and at the head of the bed were mounds of plump white pillows with pastel embroidered borders. The old-fashioned bed sat high off the floor. Elena had climbed up a little set of stairs beside the bed to reach it.

Done bouncing, Elena climbed back down and went to the big pine dresser. "Auntie Hollie has lots of pretties. Want to see?" The little girl pulled open the drawer and displayed a jumble of pastel satins, silks and lace dainties. "She says I have to wait till I'm big to wear these." The child pulled out some of the lingerie and dreamily laid her head against the soft materials.

Noel wanted to do the same thing.

But Hollie chased such thoughts from his mind when she called out, "It's not that big a house. Come on, you two. Time to make snowflakes."

He was making snowflakes? He'd rather make love. Had plans along that line by morning if Elena ever went to bed.

He was, Hollie informed him when he and Elena returned to the kitchen.

"We'll get these in the oven and then we'll write up an offer, if you've made up your mind," she said, grating a lemon rind.

They spent the next hour making snowflakes, with Hollie frying the dough-covered iron in hot oil until the snowflakes were cooked, then Noel and Elena sprinkling the snowflakes with powdered sugar.

When they were finished, Noel and Elena were dusted with powdered sugar and looked like snowflakes themselves.

When at last the cookies had cooled it was time for Elena to go to bed. She cajoled Noel into reading her a story from one of her favorite books while Hollie cleaned up the mess.

Hollie was just hanging up a dish towel when Noel returned with the news that Elena was asleep. Finally they were alone.

"At least for now," Hollie acknowledged. "So what have you decided? Are you ready to make an offer on the house on Mistletoe Lane?"

"You sure you won't sell me this one?" he asked, taking a seat at the counter, where Hollie had brought out the papers to draw up the offer. "And I'm not certain about the street name now...."

"I'm sure."

"And you really liked the house we saw—you weren't just saying you liked it to make a sale?"

"I told you—I'd buy it myself. I don't know how to say I liked it any better than that. It's a great house at a fair price. If you want a house by Christmas, it's the one to buy."

"Okay, let's make an offer," he said. "I can even live with the street name." He frowned.

Hollie was relieved, excited and sad all at once. Relieved that Noel had given up on buying her house. Excited about the commission the sale would bring her. Sad that she would no longer be seeing Noel every day. Because as much as he drove her crazy, she'd grown used to the look of him, the smell of him, his company.

And there was still the matter of that kiss.

He could have given her a peck on the cheek. He could have buzzed her lips briefly. He could even have refused.

But he hadn't. Instead he'd given her a real kiss. A very real, romantic kiss. The kind that led to... something. It hadn't been a perfunctory kiss between real estate agent and client, happily sealing a closed deal.

However, the kiss hadn't led to anything.

True, their relationship had grown more relaxed...less formal and more teasing...but it hadn't developed beyond that.

Now it was over as quickly as it had begun. She would show Noel's offer. The seller would haggle a little, maybe make one or two counteroffers before accepting Noel's price, and then Noel would be off to the islands for Christmas.

"How long do you think it's going to take to close the deal?" Noel asked, interrupting her thoughts as she filled out the offer. His romantic plans didn't fit her plan to close the deal. He was hot and she was all business.

"Why? Did you want to use the phone to call the airline and make your reservations?" He was really in a hurry to get away.

"There's that," he agreed, disappointed at his thwarted plans for the evening.

"Go ahead and call," she said, not looking at him. "With any luck, we can settle everything tomorrow. And if need be, you can finish up by phone from your island."

Without much effort, he'd managed to ruin her hope of a very Merry Christmas.

This time her daydreams had been way too fanciful. The ones she hadn't even admitted to herself.

Till now.

Meanwhile, back at the North Pole...

"HOW COULD CLAUDIA GO away and leave me nothing to eat but a freezer full of Lean Cuisines," Santa muttered, pushing away his second empty container.

Santa hated how people who reformed their bad habits lost their senses of humor. Or was his workaholic schedule the reason Claudia didn't laugh anymore the way she used to?

He went back to the test in one of Claudia's glossy women's magazines he'd been checking for a hint to

what spa she might be at. The test was to see if your
marriage was in trouble.

He finished tallying his answers and found out what
Claudia's absence had already told him.

He was going to have to make some changes.

A diamond tennis bracelet might be a good way to
start. And an indoor tennis court.

Claudia would look sexy in one of those short white
tennis skirts . . . if she came back.

8

December 23

"So HOW WAS your date with the fireman last night?" Hollie asked, sitting on Sarah's striped sofa with her stocking feet up on the oak coffee table.

"He's coming over tomorrow night to celebrate Christmas Eve with us. Why don't you bring Noel?" Sarah hinted.

"Because Noel will be long gone."

"You didn't sell him your house, Hollie, did you?"

"No, but I finally found one he liked. We put in an offer early this morning and I'm waiting to hear," she said, patting the beeper she was never without. "It's weird. One minute he's gung ho for my house—the next minute he's buying another one. Not that I'm not thrilled to get a big commission and to keep my house...but still..."

Sarah took a sip of the honey-and-lemon tea she'd made them. "Here's some dime-store analysis—for what it's worth. Have you ever considered the fact that Noel was attracted to your house because he's attracted to you? Maybe it was his way of getting you in his life—symbolically, that is."

Hollie laughed nervously. "Thanks, Ms. Freud. *If* I believe your analysis, why has he decided to buy another house?"

Sarah shrugged. "Got me there. Maybe..." She paused and gave Hollie a mischievous look. "Because he wants a house big enough for the both of you."

Hollie blushed. "Go on! I hardly know the man. He hardly knows me."

"Yeah, right." Sarah harrumphed. "You've spent day in and day out with him for over a week. What don't you know about each other? And besides...let me tell you, there's some heavy-duty intensity and spark-flying going on between the two of you. Why don't you see where it can go? Maybe it you ask real nice Noel will stay for Christmas."

"Not a chance. He's a grinch, remember? And furthermore, he can't wait to get away to a hot Caribbean island."

"Come on, Hollie. Give it a chance. And give Noel a chance. Surely a Christmas freak like you can convert him. Make him want to celebrate with us. I know Elena would like him to be there. She came home all chirpy about how Noel read her stories from the books you're constantly collecting for her."

"Did he ever read her stories!" Hollie said, with a laugh. "She kept getting up when we thought she was asleep and begging Noel to read to her. We were both falling asleep by the time she did."

"Aha, so there was *courting* going on. He lingered after you wrote up the offer. I'm sorry about Elena putting the damper on things for you two." Sarah's laugh was husky and girlish. "Well, not that sorry. Otherwise Rick and I wouldn't have been necking—"

"Sarah! It was your second date!"

"Well, I had a child with me on the first one. I couldn't very well lock lips at the *Nutcracker*."

"That's not what I meant and you know it, you hussy. You're not supposed to neck until the third date."

"Midnight, get down," Sarah scolded as the little dog snitched a snowflake cookie from the open snowman tin on the coffee table. "Tell me where it says you're not supposed to neck until the third date, Hollie."

"I know I heard it somewhere." Hollie sniffed. "Besides, Noel wasn't courting me. He was just lonely and didn't want to go back to his room. I think he gets a charge out of Elena's antics. He certainly did try to get her to sleep."

"I'll bet," Sarah said beneath her breath. "Well, I think you should at least ask him if he'll come Christmas Eve. Maybe if he has somewhere to go, he won't leave St. Louis at all."

Hollie folded up her list of things to do and put on her shoes to head out and finish her last-minute errands. "Think about it, Sarah. A sunny beach, warm sand, ocean breezes...he's not staying. And neither am I. As much as I'd like to laze away the day with you, I've places to go, crowds to shoulder through. Want me to pick up anything for you now that I'm finally officially on vacation and don't have to show Noel any more houses?''

"I'm all set. All the catering is done for now, and by the way, the Witmers were very complimentary about the dinner, thanks."

As Hollie stood to leave, her beeper went off.

"So much for the best-laid plans. It's the offer. Can I use your phone?"

"Like you have to ask. Go, girl."

SARAH RANG the doorbell on the Victorian gingerbread house. She felt Hollie could use all the help she could get, so she'd decided to pay Hollie's visionary a little visit as soon as Hollie left and while Miss Nosy Elena was still playing at a neighborhood chum's.

It had seemed like a good idea at the time, but now she felt a little foolish.

The woman who answered the door banished her reservations. Ms. Claudia was completely charming as she ushered Sarah into the living room, urging her to be seated near the fireplace.

"What is it you'd like to know?" Ms. Claudia asked, taking Sarah's hand. "Do you want to find out how your catering business is going to go, or if that sweet little Elena is going to have brothers and sisters?"

"Well, I ah—" Sarah supposed she shouldn't be surprised Ms. Claudia knew so much . . . she was a psychic.

"Oh, you want to find out about that fireman of yours, I bet, from the way you're blushing."

"He's not mine. I mean—"

"Oh, he's yours for the taking, honey." Ms. Claudia patted Sarah's hand.

"Really?"

Ms. Claudia nodded. "You do like him, don't you?"

"Yes, but he's a little..."

"You need someone younger to keep up with you and Elena. Besides, with all his brothers and sisters, he's a very mature young man."

"He does seem to be. But that's not really why I stopped by. I wanted to ask you about my friend Hollie. Hollie Winslow. She came to see you and you told her Santa was going to bring her a six-foot-one-inch beau for Christmas."

"I know she doesn't believe it, does she?"

"I believe it. I think she's already met him, but she's too stubborn to act."

Ms. Claudia leaned forward and smiled. "They're both too stubborn."

"Then how—"

"I know you want to help your friend, Sarah," Ms. Claudia interrupted. "But they have to work it out for themselves. Hollie will have to come to understand that Noel needs what she has to offer."

"There's nothing I can do?" Sarah asked, wanting to bring her friend the happiness she deserved.

"They'll work it out," Ms. Claudia assured her.

Sarah smiled. "In that case, how *is* my catering business going to do?"

"I think if your fireman has his way, you're going to be catering to him and..."

"More children!"

"If you want them."

"Elena will be thrilled. She's been pestering me for a little sister. Oh, by the way, you wouldn't know where I could get a Barbie in a pink dress, would you?"

"It's on its way."

"You mean Santa is bringing it?"

"With a little help from a courier."

Sarah looked down at her watch. "Oops, I've got to run. Elena will wonder what's happened to me."

"Merry Christmas," Ms. Claudia said, walking Sarah to the door. She smiled, knowing that Sarah's unselfish act of adopting Elena was going to pay off in the dividend of twin boys. Elena had better enjoy being a spoiled princess while she could!

As Claudia went to the kitchen to warm up some soup, she wondered what Santa was doing.

Wondered if he missed her as much as she missed him.

"CONGRATULATIONS, you've got yourself a house," Hollie said, clinking her champagne glass with Noel's.

"And without any quibbling from the owners. They took my first offer."

"You got lucky," she said, pouring him some more champagne from the bottle he'd brought with him when he arrived at her house to celebrate closing the deal.

"You're pretty gussied up," she commented, taking in his double-breasted suit and his silk tie. "You sure you didn't already start work? You haven't changed your mind about leaving town for Christmas, have you?" She tried to keep the note of hope from her voice.

"I bought a ticket for a flight that leaves tomorrow afternoon at two. I'm dressed up because I thought maybe we could go to dinner to celebrate. I've given you a pretty hard time and you deserve a good meal on me."

"Dinner?"

He nodded. "Anywhere but Honey Bear's Pizza Cave."

"I'll have to shower and change...." She knew most men hated to wait for women.

"Go ahead—we've got time. Just tell me where you want to eat and I'll call and make reservations while you get ready."

Hollie took a sip of champagne, and felt giddy from the bubbly wine. It was the champagne, wasn't it, and not the man who looked as though he'd walked off the cover of *Gentlemen's Quarterly*? She remembered Sarah talking about an elegant restaurant in Clayton with a funny name. What was the name—Crazy something? "Crazy Fish," she said. "I've been wanting to try it."

"Crazy Fish, it is. Go ahead and get ready, then," he said, draining his champagne flute and setting it on the counter.

"The phone book is in the bread drawer," she informed him, heading off to her bedroom with a wave.

After he made the call and set the reservations for two, he settled on the sofa with a refilled flute of champagne to wait. He'd allotted an hour for her to get ready and a half hour for them to reach the restaurant.

Sitting on the sofa reminded him of the snowy day he'd fallen asleep there and the sexy dream he'd had of Hollie. It had been a very vivid dream, romantic and sensual, and he was getting hot. He set down the champagne flute and walked down the hall to where he'd heard the shower running in Hollie's bathroom.

Another image came to mind.

The dresser drawer Elena had coveted and opened, much like Pandora's box. It tempted him into the bedroom.

The shower was still running, steam drifting out into the bedroom. He caught the scent of Hollie's perfumed soap. It smelled like honeysuckle and musk.

A bold desire overtook him as judgment left him. He slid open the lingerie drawer and began having a look through it. Merely professional curiosity, he told himself. After all, he was in retail.

He picked up a bra in lavish Venetian lace with dainty rosette trim, then discarded it and its matching stretch-mesh pantie in favor of a white teddy detailed with lovely eyelet embroidery and scalloped edging. It was pure and provocative, like Hollie.

Boldly, he laid it on the bed, then went to her closet and sorted through it, stopping first at a lemon pleated crepe suit. Its sunny color pleased him, but it wasn't exactly what he had in mind. Searching further, he came up with the perfect candidate for dinner at Crazy Fish: a sleek little white spandex top with a ballet neck and a midthigh-length black ribbed knit skirt.

He laid those out alongside the teddy. He looked at the ensemble speculatively, then went back to the lingerie drawer for sheer nude panty hose.

The shower was still running, and the escaping steam lent a sultry atmosphere to the room and his clandestine behavior. He was taking a chance, risking blowing the evening.

Shoes! He'd almost forgotten. She had a thing for them, so choosing them would be a real treat. The top shelves of her closet were stacked high with shoe boxes. His task was made easy by her efficient system of taping a snapshot of each pair of shoes to the end of each box.

After a quick inventory, he settled on pretty black pumps with elasticized crisscross straps and about two-inch block heels.

He slipped the shoes from their box and hurried to the bed, where he placed them alongside his other selections for the evening.

His ears perked up at the sound of the shower being turned off and the shower door sliding open. She was getting out to towel off. He lingered a second to visualize her naked, with water droplets on her smooth skin and her curls damp against her neck.

And then he moved silently from the room to wait back in the living room.

How would she react when she saw the clothes laid out on her bed?

It was true he'd invaded her privacy. And what he'd done was very intimate.

Suggestive.

Possessive.

And maybe stupid.

But if she reacted the way he hoped, he'd be able to feast on the memory in the islands over Christmas. And just knowing he'd picked out every intimate detail of her clothing would excite him terribly as he sat across from her during dinner tonight.

He didn't know why he'd done it. He had certainly never done anything like it before. Never revealed himself so recklessly.

The wait seemed forever, although just seconds passed. Had she left the bathroom yet? Had she discovered the clothing?

When she did, what would she think?

What would she do?

It was so quiet he could hear the furnace kick on and the ping against the windows of a light sleet that had begun to fall.

He got up and began pacing absently, his nerves making him restless. There was a bowl of sugared fruit on the piano. He picked a grape and plopped it into his mouth before he knew what he was doing. The sweet-tart taste only heightened his senses.

Sitting down at the piano, he began doodling on the keys, picking out a favorite song by ear. He was no more than an adequate player, but the distraction relaxed him.

He didn't hear Hollie the first time she called his name. Or the next.

The third "Noel" caught his ear.

"Are you calling me?" he asked, leaving the piano and walking down the hall toward her bedroom, hoping like hell he wasn't hearing things. Afraid his overactive imagination had conjured the sound.

"Would you come in here, please?" Hollie said as Noel walked by a framed handprint of Elena's on the wall, next to a picture of her in a ballerina outfit. He passed Elena's "room," where he'd read her bedtime stories until midnight while Hollie had painted the little girl's toenails cherry red, as promised. She spoiled the child rotten.

He wouldn't mind being spoiled rotten by her, he thought, entering the bedroom...not knowing just what to expect.

She was dressed.

In the exact ensemble he'd picked out. And she was smiling, he saw with relief. A quirky little smile of acknowledgment.

"I thought you might like," she said, opening the velvet case on her dresser, "to pick out my earrings, as

well. Then all I have to do is my hair and we'll be ready
to go."

Hell, he was ready to go!

She looked like a sexy dream in the outfit he'd selected for her. Sweet and sexy at the same time.

Was it a trap? Was she ready to blast him for the lib-
erties he'd taken? A little uncertain, he approached the
velvet box and looked inside. Every piece of jewelry was
whimsical, from angels to hearts to moons and stars.

He decided to give her what she wanted and picked up
one of the red-and-green glitter holiday wreaths. He was
close enough to see that her ears were pierced. Close
enough to want to nibble on them. For starters.

Dinner was way down on the list of what he wanted
at that moment.

She smiled at his selection.

"Do you want to put it in?" she asked.

He nearly swallowed his tongue, thinking she'd read
his mind.

She turned her pierced ear toward him, waiting, and
he realized she'd been talking about the earring in his
hand.

Tongue-tied, he did just that, fumbling only a little
with the delicate earring.

"Thanks," she said, handing him the other one. "I
touched up my manicure and didn't want to wreck it,"
she explained, blowing on her nails.

He thought the gesture interesting. She could have
been blowing on her nails to dry them, but it looked to

him as if she was congratulating herself on accomplishing something.

He was afraid to think what.

Hell, he didn't want to think at all. And then, giving in to impulse, he didn't.

Running his forefinger from the shell of her ear along her jaw, he passed the pad of his thumb over her lips and then lowered his lips to hers in a moment of spontaneous passion. He coaxed a response from her as he buried his hands in her damp curls. His tongue explored her delicious mouth with a sense of urgency.

"We're going to be late," she said when he broke the kiss.

"Do you care?" he asked.

She answered him by reaching up to kiss him back.

A kiss of invitation that made him lose control.

He swung her up into his arms without breaking the kiss and carried her across the room. She clung to his broad shoulders, breathless still from the deep, probing thrust of his tongue.

"What are you doing?" she asked when they broke apart to gasp for air.

"Your bed has fascinated me since the first moment I saw it. It looks like a floating cloud, so high off the floor. I've wanted to see if it would possibly be as soft and inviting as it looks."

Hollie squealed as he tossed her from his strong arms up on the bed.

She bounced once and then was enveloped in a tumble of plump white pillows.

Hurriedly he loosened his tie and shed it along with his suit jacket, then leaped to join her on the bed. Lying across her, he whispered in her ear, telling her about the dream he'd had about her, about what her lips had been up—er, down—to.

"Is that a request?" she asked.

"Maybe later," he replied, pushing up her skirt as she arched her hips to assist him.

He cupped her bottom as he ground against her and moaned. His fingers flicked the snaps on the white teddy and he ripped the fabric of the sheer hose easily.

She let out a gasp of pleasure when he slid down on the bed to cover her pulsing sex with his warm mouth. While she squirmed beneath him, he sucked, then alternately raked his teeth against the tender flesh, until she was moaning his name. He upped the ante when he laved her with smooth, broad strokes of his tongue that didn't penetrate only tormented, teased.

And then her hands, which had been clutching the sheets, cupped his ears, guiding him, insisting, until he furled his tongue in swirls of pleasure inside her till she shuddered against him and then went limp beneath him with exhausted passion.

He took her hand and kissed her palm, then stretched out alongside her, listening to her breathing, shallow and fast, until it returned to normal.

"Where did that come from?" Hollie asked, turning on her side and facing him, trailing her fingers over his broad chest.

"Just being a gentleman," he answered.

"A gentleman? That's an interesting way of putting it, don't you think?"

"You know, returning the favor," he explained, referring to the dream he'd had about her.

She chuckled. "Yeah..."

He stacked his hands behind his head as he eased over onto his back. His sex was hard and saluting.

It drew her hand. "So what do you think?" she asked, stroking.

"At the moment I'm incapable of thought. All the blood has left my head and gone... elsewhere."

"I mean, what do you think—is the bed as soft as you imagined? Do you like it?"

"Um..." was all he said as she squeezed the length of him with gentle command.

And then her lips replaced her hand.

"Wait, wait, wait a minute." He lifted her head. "Why don't we eat dinner first and come back later for dessert?"

She laughed, knowing he didn't really want to wait. "It's like I always tell Sarah—life is uncertain, have dessert first."

He took control then, flipping her body beneath his and holding both her hands in his. His mouth was on hers as he thrust inside her core, authoritatively and then teasingly slow. The pattern soon broke, however, and they engaged in an escalating race, before crossing the finish line together.

When she opened her eyes moments later she saw that at some point he'd managed to shed every stitch of clothing he had on, while she was still completely dressed, was even wearing her shoes.

For the first time in her life a man had made love to her with her shoes on. It was thrilling.

And somehow she believed he knew it.

He'd picked one of her most favorite pairs of shoes and had scored a hit right out of the ballpark. This was not your average man. But, then, she'd known that from the first time he'd walked into the real estate office and into her life.

And tomorrow afternoon he was probably walking out.

But she wasn't going to think about that. She was going to enjoy her holiday. He hadn't said any sweet words to get her into bed. He hadn't had to.

She'd been ready ever since that kiss at the mall.

If she got her Christmas wish, he'd change his mind and stay. But it wouldn't do to let herself believe, only to wish.

She knew in her heart she could make him have a Merry Christmas.

"I don't know about you, but I'm famished," Noel said, breaking into her thoughts as he rolled over and nearly fell out of bed, stopping himself just in time.

"I could probably find something in the pantry to nibble on," Hollie suggested.

"Oh, no. I promised you a posh dinner and it's a posh dinner you'll have. Besides, you already cooked for me once tonight."

She hid her blush by looking at the clock on the bedside table. "I think we missed our reservation."

"Then I'll make another one. I'll tell them we were detained. But first I'm going to take a shower. Why don't you laze away a few minutes?"

She wasn't going to argue with him. The bed was too soft and inviting. In a few minutes she'd get up and look for something else to wear.

Or maybe she'd just let Noel pick something out. She'd liked that. How exciting to come out of the shower and find he'd laid out the clothing he wanted her to wear. The idea of him going through her intimate apparel was sexually intoxicating. What had he thought about her penchant for frilly things?

She heard the shower start up and imagined him with the water spraying down on him, sheeting his muscular body.

She was so blissed out that she didn't hear the shower turn off. Didn't hear anything until she heard Noel's pained "Yeow!"

She shot out of bed and raced for the bathroom, thinking he'd slipped and fallen, broken something.

It was worse.

He was clutching the edge of the vanity, grimacing in pain, his face pale.

"What is it?"

"The curling iron," he gulped, his voice raspy. "I burned myself when I leaned forward—didn't know it was on."

Oh, Lord, no wonder he was pale. He'd nearly neutered himself. And then she had the wicked thought that she was glad she'd had dessert first, because it was going to be a while before...

Meanwhile, back at the North Pole...

"WE'VE GOT TO DO something," Terrell, the head elf, said to the elves he'd assembled for an emergency meeting the night before their biggest night of the year.

"But what?" a redheaded elf named Sammy asked. "Even Santa doesn't know where his wife disappeared to. She's the reason he's so glum."

"I'm sure if we put our heads together we can come up with something. He can't go out with the reindeer and sleigh tomorrow night to make all his deliveries to the good little boys and girls. He's too depressed."

"I know," Sammy said. "Elf patrol."

"Elf patrol!" the rest of the elves chorused.

The last time it had been instigated was when Rudolph had refused to lead the way just before his fawn was born. They had tracked down Clarabell, the clown, to borrow her red nose for Prancer to wear to lead the reindeer.

They stacked their hands one on top of another and sang, "All for one and one for all—everyone under four feet tall. We're on our way. It's off we go. For there is no Merry Christmas without Santa's ho, ho, ho."

The oak chest was opened and elf patrol helmets dispatched. Magic was afoot.

9

December 24

HOLLIE HADN'T REALLY known what she'd wanted for Christmas until last night, when Christmas had come early, she decided with a wicked laugh as she lazed in bed. She should get up. There were all sorts of chores vying for her attention. But she wanted to linger longer. To enjoy reliving last night—well, right up until Noel had stepped out of the shower, reached for a towel on the vanity and leaned into pain.

That had ended dinner.

The evening.

Romance.

He'd limped out, to her profuse apologies.

She pulled the pillow next to her over and hugged it tight, inhaling the scent of him, all wood smoke and fresh citrus. She was naked beneath the covers save for one accessory: the earrings he'd selected. She'd left them on when she'd undressed after Noel had left. After unplugging the curling iron and putting it in a safe place to cool down, she'd showered and gone to bed, but not to sleep.

She'd been too keyed up. She'd been with a man who'd known what he wanted and hadn't been shy about taking it and giving back. At that moment she'd bet her cheeks were as red as the glitter on her wreath earrings—or "ear bobs," as Elena called them. Lovemaking had never been so exciting as with Noel. He'd seduced her without touching her by selecting what he wanted her to wear and laying it out for her on the bed as if she were some harem girl being prepared for a pasha.

It excited her to know he'd been going through her things while she'd been naked in the shower. To wonder if he'd watched her secretly while she'd showered.

From any other man that would have been an unforgivable liberty, but Noel had done it in such a romantic way that she'd been pleased rather than angered.

A glance at the clock beside her told her she was going to have to get up no matter how delicious the lingering. But she was enjoying reliving each caress, the murmured words in a foreign language that had lent a fillip to the lovemaking, a fillip of mystery. What had he said to her? What had he said in the words that had been so full of emotion and desire?

Had he said "I love you"?

Could he have?

Her growling stomach rudely interrupted her girlish musings. They hadn't gotten to the restaurant last night, and she'd forgotten to eat. Her stomach was putting up a fuss. She stretched and sat up, and the comforter fell down to her waist, revealing her nudity.

She laughed. Noel couldn't have said anything that sounded like a commitment, wouldn't have—he hadn't even seen her breasts. She couldn't imagine. They would not have escaped the notice of any other man she'd ever dated.

That made Noel special indeed. She slipped from the bed and searched out a long white shirt, closing it with the tie Noel had forgotten.

Padding barefoot to the kitchen, she checked her answering machine to see if he'd called.

A little moue of disappointment caused her lips to pucker downward.

Hunger pangs ruled and she searched the cabinet for something to eat. Since she felt celebratory, she fixed her favorite breakfast—Belgian waffles and ice cream. The combination of hot buttery waffles and cold smooth ice cream quieted her growling stomach.

"Come on, call," she said, wiping her mouth with a napkin as she stared at the telephone that didn't ring. That was one of the things she hated about being a woman in a society that let men make all the moves—all the choices. Waiting.

The doorbell rang and her heart jumped.

Noel!

This was even better than a phone call.

She hoped he'd come to tell her he had changed his mind about going away for Christmas, so she could invite him to Sarah's later.

When she looked out the window, however, she saw she'd leaped to the wrong conclusion. There was a deliveryman coming up the walk with a package and a clipboard.

She grabbed one of the extra-festive packages of homemade Christmas cookies for a tip and opened the door, wondering who'd sent her a present.

After signing the clipboard, she exchanged her cookies and "Merry Christmas" for the package the deliveryman had brought. Before he had made it back to his truck, she had the package open. Maybe patience wasn't her strong suit at this time of year any more than it was Elena's.

It was the Barbie in the pink dress, just as Noel had promised. He'd saved the day. Elena would have been really disappointed not to get her number-one request.

When Hollie went to get wrapping paper to wrap the gift, the phone rang.

Finally.

She went to answer it.

"Auntie Hollie, Auntie Hollie, Santa's coming *tonight!*"

It wasn't Noel, but it was the next best thing—the little girl who always made her smile. "Are you sure it's tonight?" she teased. "Maybe you counted wrong."

"Nope. Mommy says it's Christmas Eve tonight. And I have to go to bed early after we put out the milk and cookies for Santa. Rick's coming over tonight, too."

"I like Rick," Hollie said, hoping Elena did, also.

"He's gots a spotted puppy at the firehouse named Shana. And Mommy says he's the one who cooks for the fire guys."

"Shana cooks for the firemen?"

"No, Auntie Hollie, a dog can't cook. Rick cooks firehouse chili and stuff. He said he'd make some for me."

"Well, I'll see you tonight, too, okay?"

"Uh-huh, and Mommy wants to talk to you."

Sarah came on the phone with the question Hollie wished she could answer.

"Is Noel coming with you tonight?"

"I don't know."

"What kind of RSVP is that? You did ask him, didn't you?"

"Uh…well, there wasn't a good time, and he had to leave early."

"What do you mean?"

Hollie relayed what had happened with the curling iron and hung up on her best friend when she wouldn't stop laughing.

Having had enough of waiting, Hollie decided to act. With every house sale, she made up a special gift basket tailored to her client, as a thank-you. She'd make one up for Noel and deliver it to his hotel room, giving her an opportunity to invite him to Sarah's. At the very least it would let her check on Noel to make sure he was okay.

Since he was leaving at two, she had to hurry. Most of the fixings for the basket were on hand. She had the iridescent paper and ribbon for a bow to wrap around the basket. All she had to do was gather up the gift items. She quickly washed and dressed and headed out.

A good bottle of wine, crackers and cheese were all gleaned at the same market. The drugstore yielded a box of neon adhesive bandages she couldn't resist adding.

By noon she had the basket assembled and was on her way to Noel's hotel.

SHE WAS DETERMINED to get in his room.

She waited until the girl who was at the desk took a break and a man replaced her. The girl would have seen right through her lie, but the man, she knew from experience, would be susceptible to her flirting.

"Excuse me, I have a surprise for my boyfriend and he isn't answering my knock on his door. Do you think he's still in his room and has maybe fallen asleep?" She gave him her best smile, meant to make him feel like a stud muffin.

"Why don't I see if he's still registered?" the desk clerk asked, helpful as could be.

"Still registered," he reported. "But he's got a seat on the airport shuttle."

She checked her watch.

"I don't want to miss seeing him and I've got his Christmas present. Do you think I could just borrow the extra key long enough to deliver it?"

"I'm not supposed to—"

She didn't let him get his refusal out. She slid her hand over his, her eyes pleading. "But it's Christmas... and I'll only be a minute. Promise."

He gave in to her, no match for her wiles. "But hurry up," he warned, "before anyone notices the key is gone." Clearly he meant the woman who worked the front desk with him.

"Back in a wink," she said, taking the key and tossing him a wink.

SHE WAS NERVOUS as she stood outside the door of Noel's room with the gift basket.

Did she look dumb?

Worse, desperate?

Maybe she should just go.

Forget about it.

Forget about Noel.

No, she'd come this far. She wasn't a quitter when she wanted something. It was what made her such a good real estate agent. She saw things through to the end, no matter how difficult they were.

Taking a deep breath, she knocked on the door.

"Noel, I—"

The woman who'd opened the door to Noel's room clearly wasn't Noel, but clearly was expecting him. From the look of shock on her face, she was just as surprised to see Hollie as Hollie was to see her.

"Who are you?" she demanded to know. "Is that a parting gift from the hotel?"

Hollie looked down at the gift basket in her grip. "No, I, ah—who are you?" she blurted out, staring at the exquisite black lace lingerie peeking out from the cotton terry robe with the hotel's insignia on its breast pocket. "Where's Noel?"

"Who wants to know?" the woman demanded in a very territorial tone.

"I'm Hollie. Hollie Winslow. I—I sold Noel his house," she found herself stammering.

"Oh, that explains the basket. You're Noel's real estate agent. That means he found a house for us!"

"'Us'?"

"I'm Marcy Walker, Noel's fiancée," the dark-haired woman explained, wriggling her huge square-cut diamond solitaire engagement ring in Hollie's face. "My flight just got in from Atlanta. Noel must have stepped out for a minute, but the maid let me in his room. I'll take that for him, if you like."

"You're going to the islands with Noel, for Christmas?"

"Yes. He can't wait to get away every December."

Of course. They were a perfect match.

She'd seen that when she'd opened the door.

She felt like a fool.

"Well, have a good trip," Hollie said, handing over the basket, suddenly wanting not to see or be seen by Noel. She couldn't get out of the hotel fast enough.

She wasn't going to cry.

She wasn't.

"All right, damn it, I am," she sobbed when she climbed inside her car.

How had this happened to her *again?*

Noel Hawksley couldn't disappoint her because she'd known he was going to disappoint her from the start. He hadn't hidden the fact that he already had one foot on a plane out of town. He hadn't hidden the fact that he hated her favorite holiday. He'd told her so up front and often.

She had a big fat commission check, a check that would buy her a new car.

She should be happy.

Noel Hawksley had done what she thought was impossible. He'd ruined Christmas for her.

And then through her tears she smiled.

She'd ruined Christmas for him, as well. She'd accidentally branded him with her curling iron last night.

He might be spending the holidays with his fiancée, but Hollie knew she herself wouldn't be far from Noel's thoughts the whole while. After the painful accident with her curling iron, he wouldn't be enjoying himself any more than she would be. And neither would Marcy, no matter her fancy lingerie.

Hollie took some comfort in that.

"AUNTIE HOLLIE, I thought you'd never get here," Elena said when she opened the door that evening. "Are those presents all for me?"

"Have you been a good little girl?" Hollie asked, taking off her coat and hanging it up.

"Yes."

"Well, then put the presents under the tree, and no peeking who they're for. And no shaking, either," she said over her shoulder as she went to find Sarah.

"Not so much red pepper," Sarah instructed Rick, who was in the kitchen cooking.

"That doesn't smell like a Christmas ham to me," Hollie said.

"Elena insisted on Rick making his firehouse chili," Sarah explained. "Christmas Eve is going to be a little unconventional."

"What else would I expect at your house?" Hollie said, and asked for an apron to help with the preparations.

"No, you're going to help me with the tree. Rick claims to have everything under control in here." Sarah steered Hollie to the boxes of lights and tree trimmings set out next to the bare tree. It was Sarah's custom to decorate her Christmas tree Christmas Eve—mainly because Midnight kept stealing the ornaments from the lower branches she could reach. And eating the tinsel. At the moment the dog was lying beneath the tree amid the presents, looking innocent.

When they were out of Rick's earshot and while Elena was peppering Rick with questions in the kitchen, Sarah whispered, "What's wrong?"

"Nothing." Hollie picked up a string of lights. "Have you tried these to make sure they're working?"

"Come on, Hollie, your eyes are puffy. You've been crying."

"I watched *Miracle on 34th Street,* okay?"

"If you say so. But what about Noel—is he coming tonight?"

Hollie shook her head and plugged in the string of lights to make sure they worked. "He's going away as planned."

"I'm sorry." Sarah touched Hollie's arm.

"It's okay. He was just a client. I sold him a house and...and..." Hollie started to sniffle.

"What is it?"

"He's engaged, Sarah." Hollie wiped her eyes and sniffed up her tears, gaining control of her emotions. She didn't want to ruin anyone's Christmas by being sad. Forcing a note of cheerfulness into her voice, she said, "And she's beautiful."

"What do you mean? How do you know?" Sarah took the lights Hollie handed her around the tree, made a pass and handed the lights back to Hollie as they circled them around the tree.

"I saw her. She was in Noel's hotel room when I delivered the thank-you basket I made him for purchasing a house from me." Hollie picked up another strand of lights and checked them at the outlet.

"Maybe she was lying."

Hollie shook her head. "She showed me her engagement ring. It was huge."

"I don't know what to say."

The doorbell ringing prevented her from saying anything. She went to answer it, but Elena raced ahead before Sarah could get there. "I'll get it," she yelled.

Hollie dropped the lights she was holding when she heard Elena squeal with delight, "Noel!"

What was he doing here? How did he have the nerve to show up to face her? He must know she'd discovered his little secret.

She didn't want to see him. Didn't want him to see her. She rubbed her eyes.

Sarah came to fetch her.

"He wants to see you, Hollie," she said, knowing Hollie would have heard Elena.

"Tell him no."

Elena came running in with a small, gaily wrapped box. "Noel brought me a present!"

"Put it under the tree, honey," Sarah instructed, her eyes pleading with Hollie. "At least talk to him," she said.

Not wanting to make a scene and ruin the evening, Hollie agreed and went to the door, where Noel was waiting to see her.

"Can I come in?" he asked.

"No. I'll come out." She reached for her coat and slipped into it, going outside to join him.

"Hollie, you've got to let me explain."

She didn't answer him at first, biting her lower lip to keep from blurting out her hurt. Finally she said, "I don't think you can give me a satisfactory explanation, Noel. Anyway, it's your fiancée you owe the apology to, not me. She's the one with the claim on you, with your ring on her finger. I saw the ring, Noel. You aren't really going to stand there and tell me it's not your engagement ring she had on, are you?''

"It's my ring," he agreed. "But—"

"Goodbye, Noel." She turned to go back inside, but he grabbed her arm.

"Wait, Hollie, you have to listen. At least hear me out. You're wrong about—"

Rick, who had apparently been watching from the kitchen window, opened the door. "Is everything all right out here, Hollie?" he asked, concern and protection in his voice.

"Yes, I'm fine," she told him.

He went back inside, leaving them alone.

"What you don't understand is that Marcy Walker is my ex-fiancée."

"So you had a little fight. I'm sure you'll patch it up. Meanwhile I have a life to get back to," Hollie said, looking at his hand on her arm.

He released his hand.

"No, you aren't listening to me, Hollie. I wouldn't have slept with you last night if I was still engaged to Marcy. She broke our engagement on Christmas Eve— last year. It seems that now she thinks she made a mistake and wants us to give it another try."

"And I think you should," she lied, shaking off a gust of cold wind that made the pine tree by the mailbox shiver.

"Hollie, you're being unreasonable. Why won't you listen to what I'm trying to tell you?" he pleaded, his hands shoved in his pockets so he wouldn't grab her again.

"I know what I saw, Noel. I came to your hotel to ask you here tonight, to try to convince you that running away wasn't the answer. But when I got to your room I saw that you weren't running away, but toward another woman. A half-dressed woman in *your* hotel room wearing *your* engagement ring. There isn't any spin you can put on that that I will believe. I think you should just go, please."

"Maybe you're right. I never did have much luck this time of year." He turned and walked away toward his car.

It took everything Hollie had not to run after him and stop him. But she didn't want just any man. She wanted a man who wouldn't disappoint her. A man she could believe in.

When Hollie went back inside, Sarah was setting the table and Elena was hanging tinsel on the tree as Midnight danced at her feet, trying to snag some.

"What can I do to help?" Hollie asked, forcing a note of brightness into her voice.

"Here, you can mix the salad," Rick offered. "On second thought, I'll do the salad and you chop the onions to go on top of the chili with the shredded cheese."

Hollie knew he'd offered her the onion job because there were tears in her eyes and chopping onions would help her hide the reason for them. Sarah had found herself a real catch. She hoped her friend realized it.

The rest of the evening went downhill from there.

Rick and Sarah were so smitten with each other that it was painful for Hollie to be around them. But she was a good friend, and complimented Rick on his cooking, made happy conversation with Elena and tried to assure Sarah with her eyes that she was fine.

She only had one second of doubt about her decision to send Noel away.

It was the moment Elena pestered her about when Noel was coming back and why he'd left without eating.

When Hollie explained that he'd only come by to say goodbye before he left on his vacation, Elena asked permission to open the present he'd left for her.

To defuse the situation, Sarah had agreed that Elena could open her present from Noel.

Hollie almost began crying again when she saw what the gift was. Somewhere he had managed to find a set of stack rings small enough for a child's finger. Elena was so excited she danced around showing everyone her jewels.

Right after that Hollie took her leave.

Setting up milk and cookies for Santa was something Rick and Sarah could share. She didn't belong.

For the first time Hollie felt really alone, even though she'd been alone all her life.

She didn't even bother to turn on her Christmas lights when she got home. Darkness welcomed her and she embraced it.

CLAUDIA CLAUS RUBBED her temples.

She had made a mess of things. She thought she'd read the manual that came with Santa's laptop, but somewhere along the line she must have done something wrong. After all, Santa used the computer to make children's Christmas dreams come true. All he did was type the wish into the computer and it was a done deal.

Perhaps she shouldn't have interfered in Hollie's life.

She had made Hollie miserable. She'd been so sure that Noel was the right one for her. Had been so sure that they were soul mates.

Both deserved their share of happiness.

Santa was not going to be happy with her when he found out she'd taken the special laptop and made a mess of things. She couldn't go back to the North Pole for Christmas having failed at her first project.

What had gone wrong? She'd spent years reading romance novels and dearly loved a happy ending.

Totally believed in them.

She should have started out smaller, worked on a first crush, an infatuation or something like that. It would have been like using training wheels to learn how to ride a bike.

True love was the big one and she was an amateur. Santa made it all look so easy, making everyone happy.

She'd found out it was easy to make someone cry.

Making them laugh—now that was the hard ticket. But she *would* do it. She still had time to make true love happen before Christmas was over.

She reread the manual.

And realized she'd forgotten to press Save.

She pressed the button to save Hollie's Christmas.

Meanwhile, back at the North Pole...

"TIME TO GO, Santa," Terrell said, checking his watch.

"I suppose." Santa sighed, taking his red suit from the head elf.

When he was all dressed, down to his polished black boots, Terrell walked with Santa out to the sleigh, where the reindeer were stamping impatiently, excited to begin their long flight. They'd made bets as usual about the length of time it would take them to make the trip.

Prancer never won, but he always came back with the fullest tummy. He had a nose for sniffing out who put a bunch of fresh carrots on their doorstep for the reindeer.

When Santa was settled into his sleigh and the sacks of toys were secured—the magic, bottomless sacks—Terrell took a piece of paper from his pocket. "This is for you, Santa," he said, handing it over.

"What is it—another name to add to the list of toy deliveries?"

"No, it's where Mrs. Claus is staying."

"You found her!"

Terrell nodded. "And, sir, there's a picnic basket in the back with a romantic dinner for two. I thought you might want to have a late-night snack with your wife...."

10

December 25

HOLLIE WAS DISAPPOINTED in herself when she woke up Christmas morning with raccoon eyes, having gone to bed and cried herself to sleep.

She shoved the covers off and went to take a shower, having had enough of feeling sorry for herself. It was self-indulgent and she was having none of it. She was taking her holiday back. Putting the Merry back in Christmas. Taking control.

Noel might have discombobulated her and derailed her and swept her off her feet and crashed her over a romantic cliff, but she was a survivor.

It was a day for fresh starts, believing in miracles and loving someone, even if it was only yourself.

After a breakfast of angel cookies and hot chocolate, she went out to get her mail, which she'd forgotten yesterday.

When she reached the mailbox, she found that it contained a surprise. Someone had left her a posy. A completely charming gesture. The arrangement was made up of apricot tulips, veronica, bouvardia and hypericum, and at this time of year had to have cost the earth.

Enchanted, she pulled the arrangement from the mailbox. Holding it where it was tied with a big red bow, she plucked the small white card and read: Merry Christmas.

The flowers hadn't been left that long ago. They weren't wilted from the cold. She looked around to see if a car was parked nearby, but there was none. Whoever had left them was gone.

And then she dropped the card, and when it fluttered to the ground it landed facedown. On the back Noel had scrawled his name.

He'd just been here.

She'd just missed him.

Why couldn't Ms. Claudia have left well enough alone? Why did she have to bring her a six-foot-one-inch grinch to break her heart?

She wouldn't think about him.

She wouldn't.

Once inside, she almost tossed the posy in the trash, but at the last second popped it in a small vase of water, instead.

It dawned on her suddenly what the fresh flowers meant.

Noel hadn't gone to the Caribbean with Marcy. Hadn't gone to the islands at all.

What did that mean?

She pushed the doubts from her mind, turned on the stereo system and put on her favorite CD of carols.

Then she lost herself in work, cleaning out her brief-case. When she had all her paperwork neat and tidy, she realized that her key was missing once again.

But this time it couldn't be Elena who'd lifted it. She must have left it at the house Noel had bought on Mis-tletoe Lane. It was the last time she remembered hav-ing it.

The owners would be back in the morning, so she needed to go to the house and hope she'd left some-thing unlocked so she could retrieve the key.

She wanted to get out of the house anyway. There were too many memories of Noel being in her home. So she got dressed in warmer clothes and headed out.

Christmas was the quietest day of the year.

The streets were deserted as she drove to the house. She thought of Elena and wondered if she'd liked her Barbie in pink. She'd have to call her when she got home and share the excitement of Christmas morning with her over the phone.

Noel's luxury car parked outside the house when she pulled up the drive was a surprise.

She must have left the key with him.

Her first instinct was to leave. But she couldn't leave because she had to retrieve the key. So she got out of her car and walked up to the house.

She tried the door before knocking. It was open.

Should she go in? Maybe Noel was here with Marcy. Maybe he was showing her around the house he'd bought for her. She didn't know if she could handle seeing that.

But she needed the key. So she opened the door and went inside.

"Is anyone here?" she called out.

No answer.

It was very quiet in the house. Maybe he was looking around outside. She twisted her hands together nervously.

She could do this, she promised herself.

Taking a deep breath, she headed for the kitchen, which was the most likely place Noel would have set down the key. However, she didn't make it to the kitchen.

Instead she stopped in her tracks when she saw Noel sitting on the floor in front of the empty fireplace. He was staring at the diamond ring he held in his fingers.

She cleared her throat. "I came for the key," she said.

He looked up in surprise. "It's on the kitchen counter." He nodded toward the kitchen, which adjoined the dining room.

"What do you do, buy a woman an engagement ring every Christmas? Is that how you get your kicks?" she couldn't resist accusing.

"No, not this year. I told you this is last year's ring. I told Marcy to keep it, but when it became clear to her that I wasn't interested in having her back, she threw it at me and left."

"I see." Could he be telling her the truth? She wanted desperately to believe him. Finding Marcy half-undressed in his room had been a shock, a terrible blow to her self-confidence.

"Did you know I bought this house for you?" he asked, searching her face for some sign that he hadn't been wrong about them.

"What?"

"That was why I wanted to know, wanted to be sure you loved it. I wanted us to be happy in it. As happy as you are in the little house you now have. I wanted us to raise a family in it. You see, Hollie, I realized when I saw your house that I wasn't looking for a house at all." He hesitated. "I was looking for a home."

And she was crying again. "Oh, No-oel—"

He got to his feet then and gathered her in his arms.

"Oh, Hollie. I thought I was done taking risks in my personal life. But once I met you I didn't have any choice. It was as if someone picked you out for me personally. Someone who knew who my fantasy soul mate was."

Hollie let Noel wipe her tears away with the pads of his thumbs as he vowed, "I want you. I need you. I love you, Hollie. Please put your magic in my life. I didn't know how alone I could feel until I thought I was losing you. We belong together, Hollie. Like apple pie and ice cream, like Hootie and the Blowfish, like Christmas and Santa Claus."

She smiled at the last. "There's never any mistletoe when you need it," she sniffed.

"Hell, we're on Mistletoe Lane, sweetheart," Noel said, laying on a kiss that made Ms. Claudia sigh.

Happy endings were the *best*.

Meanwhile, back at the North Pole...

"I'VE MISSED YOU terribly," Santa said, caressing Claudia's cheek.

"You mean you weren't too busy to notice I was gone?"

"You're my wife. How could you think I wouldn't miss you?" Santa asked, hugging her.

"Oh, my, is it me, or have you lost weight?" Claudia asked.

"I've been pining away for you."

"Then you didn't find where I hid the Christmas cookies...." Claudia Claus chuckled. She got up and promised to be right back with a surprise for him.

When she returned she had a big tin of homemade Christmas cookies and a six-pack of micro brewery beer.

"Where did you get them?" Santa asked when she sat back down beside him in front of the fire.

She handed him a cold bottle of "Santa's Suds," as the label on the long-necked beer bottle said, and took one for herself. "I had the beer made special for you at a small brewery in St. Louis. And the cookies were hidden in the box the treadmill came in. If you had set it up to use, as you promised, you would have found them."

Santa clinked his glass to Claudia's and toasted with a twinkle in his eye, "To my wife, I promise to set up the treadmill and never to take you for granted again."

"And to use the treadmill," Claudia added, as they both took a sip.

"Now I have a present for you," Santa said, slipping a small package from his pocket.

"What is it?" Claudia cried in delight.

"Open it and find out."

She unwrapped the package with a speed that rivaled Elena's. "Oh, Santa! It's beautiful."

"There's going to be a tennis court to go with it. That way we can exercise together."

"And have a love match," Claudia said with a sigh.

"Ho, ho, ho."

11

"BUT THE STORES are closed," Hollie said as Noel pulled into the parking lot of the posh mall where the new store he was opening was located.

"I know," Noel replied as they sat there outside the south end of the mall, the engine of his luxury car purring. "But I have a key to the store."

"You mean you have to work? I thought we were going to celebrate Valentine's Day." There was a hint of a sulk in her voice.

"I'm not working. Everything is ready for tomorrow's grand opening. But before the store opens in the morning, I thought the two of us could celebrate my favorite holiday here with plenty of privacy."

"Not an easy thing to find at ten-thirty on a Friday night, I agree," Hollie said, warming to the idea.

"Well, you were the one who had to work late writing up a contract for a client. Tonight was one of my early nights. But that was okay, because it gave me time to set this up."

"Set what up?"

"You'll see."

Hollie was giddy with excitement as Noel escorted her into the closed mall. There was something sexy and exciting about their clandestine entry into the upscale department store he was opening. He had overseen every detail of the store until it was perfect.

"Come on," he said, tugging her along when she would have lingered to look at every little thing. She and Sarah had been more likely to haunt flea markets and tag sales than do posh shopping. The only big purchase she'd made recently was the new car she'd bought using the commission check as a down payment.

Noel had been introducing her to a whole new world since they'd begun dating at Christmas. A world she'd known existed, of course, but one she'd not really had access to. It was sort of like a fairy tale. One with a happy ending. Noel had been talking about marriage, and although they were both scared, they were in love.

"You really did set this up," Hollie said when they stopped at the fine jewelry counter and a bottle of chilled champagne and two glasses were set out on a tray, waiting for them.

"I told you it was my favorite holiday," Noel said. The store was decorated with splashes of red to draw the eye to special displays and offers for the grand opening.

He went behind the counter and played host, pouring champagne into the two glasses after a showy pop of the cork and the bubbly flow of champagne, which he'd caught with a towel.

"To us," he said, offering her a glass.

She giggled at the bubbles that tickled her nose when she took a sip.

"Remember what happened the last time we had champagne," she warned.

"I was hoping you did. Only this time I've locked up all the curling irons," he teased.

"Noel!"

"It's okay. I'm as good as new, no permanent damage done. The doctor gave me the A-OK yesterday."

"Good news," she toasted.

"See anything you like?" he asked, grinning.

She leaned over the counter and pulled him toward her with his tie. "Yeah, sweetie, you."

"I meant in a solitaire...."

"Oh—" She paused in her lean to kiss him, then looked down at the case. "You mean?"

"You are going to make an honest man of me, aren't you?"

She let go of his tie and gave the case of diamond engagement rings some serious consideration.

"Pick any one you want," he said.

"For tonight or to keep?" she asked, gazing up at him to see his true intention.

"If I give you an engagement ring, I mean for you never to take it off." She trusted the love she saw in his eyes.

Returning her attention to the rings, she pointed to a square-cut stone in a simple setting. He took it out and slipped it on her finger.

"It fits," she squealed with delight.

"Now, take your time, make sure. You can try on other rings."

"Not me," she assured him. "When something fits, I know it. This is the one."

"Come on," he said, grabbing her hand.

"Where to?"

"You'll see." He took her over to the escalator and they went upstairs to the bridal department.

"You don't expect me to pick out a wedding dress tonight, do you?"

"No. I have a surprise for you.

"Sit down here," he instructed, indicating a plush ottoman. "Close your eyes and I'll be right back with it."

As she sat there with her eyes closed, she wondered what Noel was up to. The past weeks had shown her that he was a true romantic beneath his dark, brooding looks.

"Keep your eyes closed," he said when he returned with her surprise.

She heard him kneel before her. Then heard the rustle of tissue as he opened a box.

"What is it?" she coaxed.

"Just put your foot here on my knee," he instructed, lifting it there. He then slipped off her pump and gently massaged her foot a moment.

"My surprise is a foot massage?" she guessed. "Not that I'm complaining—don't stop."

But he did stop to slip on another shoe.

"You can open your eyes now."

When she did, tears formed in the corners of her eyes. "They're beautiful," she sniffed, staring at the wedding shoes he'd had made especially for her. They were white brocade, elaborately adorned with pearl beading and Austrian crystals.

"So you like them, then?"

"Like them? I love them. I'm going to have to keep them under lock and key when Elena comes over. They look like shoes made for a princess."

"They were made for a princess," he said, slipping the other shoe on. "While I'm on bended knee, there's something I want to ask you. Will you marry me, Hollie, and make all my Christmases merry?"

"Yes, I'll marry you, Noel. You may kiss your fiancée."

He rose then from his kneeling position and made her very happy she'd said yes with a kiss fit for a princess wearing slippers that fit to perfection.

"Try walking to see if they feel okay," he suggested. "That way if there is a problem I can have them—"

"No, it's bad luck to wear them before the wedding. They're fine. They feel wonderful." She slipped them off, put them back in the tissue paper and closed the white box.

"Now, I have one last surprise for you," Noel said, tucking the box beneath his arm and motioning for her to follow him.

She tagged after him until he stopped one floor up in the sporting goods department.

"Why are we stopping here?" she asked, puzzled.

"I thought we'd go camping."

"Camping? I hate camping."

"You'll like this. Trust me. I'm doing pretty good so far, aren't I?"

A lot better than pretty good. He was making magic. He was magic. He'd put her under a spell. One she didn't want to break.

But *camping?*

He held out his hand for her.

And she said yes, unable to deny him.

He led her to an enclosed tent that was set up for display. It was the size of a large pup tent. Unzipping the flap, he motioned her inside.

She leaned forward and let out a gasp.

Inside the tent were red heart-shaped balloons blown up and floating. And a dish of chocolate-dipped strawberries on a little folding table. It was so romantic. She almost didn't hear the flap being closed when Noel ducked into the tent with her.

"Did you get any work done today?" she asked, reaching for a strawberry.

"I did this on the sly, just as the store closed. No one can ever find out. It's our little secret."

"I'm not telling," she said, savoring the chocolate-covered strawberry.

"Don't you think I deserve a little treat myself?" he asked, pulling her into his arms, kissing her a seductive let's-make-love-right-now kiss.

"You mean here?"

He murmured that he did.

"Now?"

He murmured that he did.

"But—"

"We're alone and it's raining outside. Don't you hear the rain on the tent? Doesn't it make you feel romantic?"

She did. And it did.

"Can't go camping in a tie," she said, undoing the knot and removing the tie from around his neck.

"Or a jacket," he said, pushing hers off her shoulders and letting it fall to the floor of the tent.

"I've been waiting weeks for this," he said.

"You've been planning this for weeks?"

"Uh-huh. And waiting to heal."

"You must be very frustrated."

"Very." He began undoing the vest she'd worn alone under the jacket, kissing her temples as he did so. When he had it unbuttoned, he pushed it aside and reached to free her breast from the cup of her bra, taking it full into his mouth, his tongue swirling over her nipple, making it bud into a pearl.

"This feels so wicked," she said, her hands busy freeing the buckle of his belt.

"I know," he answered, undoing the clasp at the front of her sheer blush bra so that he had access to the full playground.

She pulled his belt from the loops and dropped it to the floor, moaning at the caress of his hands and mouth on her as he eased her to the floor.

"I want you naked beneath me," he said, earnestly undressing her, hurrying.

She was equally hot. Equally ready.

Equally frustrated.

Her hands moved to free him of his shirt, while he worked at his trousers, until they were both naked and entwined limb to limb, lips to lips, heart to heart.

She could feel him hard and insistent against her hip. His tongue was mimicking what he wanted, exploring her mouth with sweet promise.

"I can't wait any longer," he rasped.

"Now," she said, and he slid into her, just as they heard voices and froze.

"I think we'll set up right here, Jonathon. Is that all right with you, Mr. Baker?" said someone from outside.

"Damn."

"What is it? Who are they?"

"It's the store manager. I completely forgot that channel five television was doing a spot for the news tonight about the grand opening."

"You forgot!" she whispered, feeling herself flush all over beneath him.

"I was busy with other things on my mind," he murmured, not moving a muscle.

Just then they heard another voice.

"This is Chriss Meyer with Channel Five at the new Bon Marché, which will open its doors in St. Louis tomorrow morning at ten o'clock. We're in the store now and—"

Hollie felt Noel begin moving inside her.

"What are you doing?" she whispered into his ear, trying not to feel how good it felt. "Are you crazy?"

"I have to, Hollie. *I have to.*"

"Noel!" she persisted, trying to still him.

"Just don't yell out my name or anything," he said, as he ignored her efforts to stop him and began moving in full thrust. "Don't scream, or we'll be on the news at eleven."

Hollie had to use all her willpower not to.

And it was worth every terrifying, thrilling second, as she heard Chriss continue talking in the background, describing the store, while she herself prayed that no one would decide to demonstrate the size of the tent and open the flap.

Noel finally collapsed after one last deep thrust that took them both over the top, with both of them holding their hands over each other's mouths.

"Happy Valentine's Day, sweetheart," he murmured, breathless.

Hollie didn't answer. She was too busy planning to get even.

At Christmas.

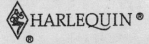

Ring in the New Year with babies, families and romance!

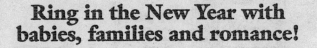

As Seen on TV!

Free Gift Offer

With a Free Gift proof-of-purchase
from any Harlequin® book, you can receive
a beautiful cubic zirconia pendant.

This stunning marquise-shaped stone is a genuine cubic
zirconia—accented by an 18" gold tone necklace.
(Approximate retail value $19.95)

Send for yours today...
compliments of HARLEQUIN®

To receive your free gift, a cubic zirconia pendant, send us one original proof-of-purchase, photocopies not accepted, from the back of any Harlequin Romance®, Harlequin Presents®, Harlequin Temptation®, Harlequin Superromance®, Harlequin Intrigue®, Harlequin American Romance®, or Harlequin Historicals® title available in August, September or October at your favorite retail outlet, together with the Free Gift Certificate, plus a check or money order for $1.65 U.S./$2.15 CAN. (do not send cash) to cover postage and handling, payable to Harlequin Free Gift Offer. We will send you the specified gift. Allow 6 to 8 weeks for delivery. Offer good until December 31, 1996, or while quantities last. Offer valid in the U.S. and Canada only.

Free Gift Certificate

Name: _____

Address: _____

City: _____ State/Province: _____ Zip/Postal Code: _____

Mail this certificate, one proof-of-purchase and a check or money order for postage and handling to: HARLEQUIN FREE GIFT OFFER 1996. In the U.S.: 3010 Walden Avenue, P.O. Box 9071, Buffalo NY 14269-9057. In Canada: P.O. Box 604, Fort Erie, Ontario L2Z 5X3.

FREE GIFT OFFER   084-KMFR

ONE PROOF-OF-PURCHASE
To collect your fabulous FREE GIFT, a cubic zirconia pendant, you must include this
original proof-of-purchase for each gift with the properly completed Free Gift Certificate.

1997
Reader's Engagement Book
A calendar of important dates
and anniversaries for readers to use!

Informative and entertaining—with notable
dates and trivia highlighted throughout the year.

Handy, convenient, pocketbook size to help you
keep track of your own personal important dates.

Added bonus—contains $5.00 worth of coupons
for upcoming Harlequin and Silhouette books.
This calendar more than pays for itself!

 Available beginning in November at
your favorite retail outlet.

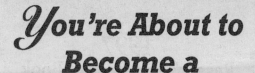

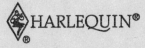